BLOOD BOUNTY

CHARMSLINGER, BOOK 1

LIZA STREET

Blood Bounty, Charmslinger, Book 1

by Liza Street

Cover designed by Keira Blackwood.

ONE

I SLAM my bag down on the bar. The barkeep and three cowherds all look up sharply at the sound. Blood seeps through the canvas, staining the bag black and coloring the bar's splintered wood.

"You can't bring that head in here," the barkeep says, handlebar mustache twitching indignantly with each word.

I'm not sure if his indignation is from the fact I'm a woman wearing trousers, the fact I'm clearly a charm-slinger from the beads on my wrist, or the fact I've set a bloody head on his bar top.

"Hell I can't," I say. "The marshal promised me a bounty if I found his vampire. Only Marshal ain't at the jail where he belongs, and he ain't here in the saloon. He ain't at home with his wife. That leaves one place—the brothel. Guess where's the one place in this sad little town I can't go?"

Sad little town is an accurate description of Shepherd, but gauging from the looks on the cowherds' faces, they don't take kindly to someone insulting their home.

One of the cowherds at the table nearby starts to stand up, his fingers going for his holster.

"Don't even think about it," I say, flicking a glance at him. "Got a charm in my holster that'll knock you blind faster than any bullet you have loaded in your grimy pistol."

The barkeep holds up a hand and the cowherd sits back down, muttering curses about the Rift and how it should swallow me whole.

"Ma'am," the barkeep says, "I'll fetch the marshal if you take the head outside."

I give him a long look, trying to suss out his truthfulness. He seems sincere enough, despite the "ma'am," which I can't tell whether or not he means ironically, given I'm obviously of mixed heritage and sling magic and charms to earn my gold, and that kind of background rarely garners respect in these parts.

But he's got to know I can hex this entire establishment fairly simply with the goodies hidden on my person. That might inspire some honesty.

"I'll be right outside, then," I say, spinning around to march back out of the saloon. My boots clomp on the wood floor and I try not to wince. I have a monster headache—residue from all the magic I had to use to bag the bloodsucker's head. A human dabbling in witch magic never has an easy time of it, but the gold from bounty hunting keeps my horse fed and gets me new boots occasionally, so I put up with the aches.

Better I use witch magic than demon or fae magic.

The demons are after your soul, the fae after your flesh. Witches just want your gold.

Outside, the stars are bright against the ink-black sky. An early summer breeze lifts the hem of my duster, letting it swirl about my legs. I lean against the wood siding of the saloon and swing my canvas sack back and forth. A little blood flings out with each rotation.

A kid scampers down the street from the side door of the saloon. Barkeep's errand boy, likely. I watch as he knocks on the brothel door. They don't let him in, either, which is a relief as there are probably things going on in there no child should be privy to. A few minutes later, a tall, thin man steps out of the brothel. That'll be the marshal. The boy speaks to him and points to where I stand in front of the saloon. I lift the canvas bag and give the marshal a finger wave.

The marshal hurries over and stops in front of me. His shirt is untucked and I feel my lip curl in disgust.

"Miss Gracie Boswell," he says as he looks me up and down. "I didn't think you'd finish so fast."

"There are bounties beyond here to collect," I say with a shrug that lifts the canvas bag up high enough to remind him I'm holding it.

"We owe you a debt. This is the bloodsucker what killed the preacher's daughter?" he asks.

I nod. "The very one. He had this in his coffin."

When I hold up a pale blue ribbon with white daisies embroidered on it, the marshal nods, his mustache lifting up and down.

"Any sign of the daughter?" he asks.

I shake my head. New vampires go straight to their

sires when they rise. "If she didn't remain with her sire, she's long gone. New vamps don't like sticking close to their old homes. It reminds them of their former humanity."

"That'll be a small comfort to the preacher." The marshal gestures toward the swinging saloon doors. "Come on in, let me buy you a drink."

"The gold owed me would be sufficient, and I'll be on my way in the morning," I say.

"But you'll want your meal," he says with a frown. "We'll have a banquet tomorrow, to honor your job well done."

"I've got grub in my saddlebags, enough to get me to the next job," I say. "Just need to find the local witch and replenish my charms."

"Please," he says, and I almost forget for a moment that he was hiding at the brothel because his tone is so kind, respectful. "You're a stranger to these parts and we'd love to show our appreciation."

I highly doubt the cantankerous barkeep and the ornery cowherds in the saloon are all that eager to appreciate me, so I tip my hat at the marshal, hand him the canvas bag with the vampire's head, and say, "Thank you kindly, but if I could just get that gold and directions to your witch, I'll be on my way."

He sighs. "Follow me, then."

We trudge along the plank walkway. Not too many people are out and about after dark. Smart. Still, there are a handful—ranchers in town to spend their gold on ale, women, and charms to keep their cattle breeding. One lone figure wearing a dress hurries along the planked walkway, a shawl draped over her head. My guess is she's fae and wearing a glamour to sneak past the marshal's attention. I see her because of the sight charm draped around my neck, but neither of us has a quarrel with the other, so I don't mention her presence.

The marshal senses something amiss and he scrunches his shoulders like a cat trying to shake off raindrops. He mutters a few words, probably a random blessing taught him by his ma, and hurries forward.

A woman leans out of one of the brothel windows. Patrolling the periphery of the building is a heavyset man wearing a duster like mine. His hat's pulled low, his hand hidden beneath his jacket. He's security, I suspect, and my suspicions are confirmed when he yells at the woman to close the damn window before someone climbs in and bleeds her dry.

"Hard to get the business if I can't show off the wares," she snaps before slamming the window shut.

"You have an infestation of bloodsuckers here?" I ask the marshal.

"Naw, just the one vampire, and you got him. There's some trouble with the fae, that's all. You take on bounties for fae?"

"No, sir," I say. I've taken on fae twice before and I'm still living to tell about it, but both encounters left me with a foot in the grave and crying to my dead ma. "I deal strictly with vampires."

He doesn't seem too bothered, and he shouldn't be. Another bounty hunter will saddle in shortly, no doubt, eager to earn some gold and prove their mettle. I wish them luck.

"That there's the witch's general store," the marshal says, pointing.

Fingers of light stream through the shuttered windows, so the hag'll still be awake. Excellent.

I stop and turn to the marshal. "Then I'll thank you kindly for my gold, and find my way out of town in the morning."

"Uh, see, that's the thing," he says. "Wasn't expectin' you to get the bloodsucker so fast. I'm a little short on funds."

I let out a sigh of exasperation. Isn't this the tale, eight times out of ten? And seven times out of those eight times, it's a bald-faced lie.

"Empty your pockets, Marshal," I say.

He narrows his eyes. "I don't think so, charmslinger."

He means it as an insult, as most people do, because magic-wielding humans ain't respectable. I don't take it as an insult, but I don't appreciate his tone, either.

"Funny you should mention my charms," I say, pasting a sweet smile on my face. "Got one in here that'll shrink your prick right down to the size of my pinkie fingernail."

He squints at me a few seconds before deciding I'm serious, then he visibly blanches. Muttering curses about charmslingers and uppity women—two insults I take gladly in stride—he fishes some gold from his pocket and shoves it into my outstretched palm. I count the coins, then raise my eyebrows at him. He shorted me.

Cursing some more, and louder this time, he places the balance into my hand.

"You know, word travels fast around these parts about

the charmslingers who take advantage of law-abiding, peaceful towns," he says. "Faster still when that charm-slinger's a woman."

"Word travels just as fast among the charmslingers about which 'peaceful' towns neglect to pay their boun-ties," I retort. "You mentioned a fae problem. Might be hard for Shepherd to get that resolved if no bounty hunter thinks you're good for the gold."

"Not everyone's aimin' to profit off of folks' troubles. We could find a respectable human who don't stoop to slinging charms," he says.

"You try that, let me know how it goes," I say pleas-antly. Plenty of the people hunting outlaws do their work with the force of plain old bullets and un-charmed stakes. Plenty more of 'em die, too.

The marshal turns to go, and the canvas sack in his hand leaks a few more drops of blood. He stops, spins around, holds up the sack. "Do I need to burn this?"

"No," I say.

"I heard a vampire needs to be decapitated and burned to keep it from rising again."

"That's an extra superstition," I say, even though I am loath to extend our conversation.

"But what about necromancy?"

The fear is evident in his tone. This marshal don't know much about outlaws. Not too much of a surprise, as this town ain't all that close to the Rift.

Taking pity on him—not that he deserves it—I say, "A necromancer could bring back a body only with the head attached. You could burn a whole body, too, and not decapitate it, to keep a necromancer from bringing it back. But it ain't necessary to do both. Trust me, this one's deader than dead. I don't want to have to come back here and kill him again."

"Thank you," he says. "It's a kindness that you explained this to me."

I shrug. I'm a charmslinger, not a monster. Although to plenty of people around here, those two things are one and the same.

TWO

THE WITCH DOESN'T LIKE me much more than the marshal did, but her dislike is subtle, and all she does is sniff loudly when I walk in. I tip my hat and remove it.

Like vampires, demons, shapeshifters, and fae, witches are considered "outlaws." But unlike the rest of them, witches have found a way to coexist with humans, mostly by offering their magic to the few souls brave enough to risk censure from other humans.

"You're hurting," the witch says, and reaches beneath her counter before bustling toward me.

She doesn't look like she intends me harm, so I hold still.

"Drink this," she says, shoving a cup of something smelly in my face.

I pick up notes of agrimony and chamomile and determine the concoction safe enough.

"Don't look so suspicious, little human," she says.

Her unwrinkled face barely moves as she talks, and her blond hair falls in loose curls down her back. I wonder how old she is. Hard to tell with witches. She could be forty-five, or eighty-five. Hell, if she were a hundred eighty-five, it wouldn't surprise me none.

She goes on, "I can see the pinch between your eyebrows. You're suffering a magic come-down, ain't ya?"

"I am," I say, taking a sip from the cup. The liquid is room temperature and tastes briny like I imagine my horse's sweat would taste, but as soon as it slides down my throat, some of the pressure behind my forehead eases. I quickly gulp down another sip. "I owe you my thanks."

"It ain't nothin'. What are you after tonight?" she asks, gesturing at the wooden trays lined up behind her counter. Bunches of dried herbs and other plants are tied with ribbons and dangle from the ceiling.

"Healing charms, and a refresh on my sight charm. Just got paid and wouldn't mind a few extra stakes if you have some good ones handy."

"I can do all that," she says. "Let me show you what I have. Healing charms first."

She pulls out one of the larger trays on the bottom. The tray is divided into smaller squares, little boxes, each one filled with charms. Some are smooth rocks that I know have been coated in resins and potions. There are some potions held in tiny glass vials. Potions packaged like that are fine if you're doing your healing at home, not so great for transporting through the hills and plains.

To solve that particular hindrance, witches also sell mending stones. They're good for smallish things like cuts, broken bones, even rattler bites.

But sometimes a mending stone ain't enough. Stronger healing charms are made with strings of stone and bone beads, with magic-imbued knots in between each bead. I wear two strings of those on my left wrist. They're my last resort charms, the most powerful I have. I could be bleeding from a hex taking my leg off at the knee and I wouldn't use one of these bracelets. I didn't even use them when my fae opponents made me cry for my ma. They ain't for one foot in the grave—they're for both feet in the grave and the dirt piling up to my waist and higher.

The shiny stones on one of the strings catch my eye. The charm looks pricey, but I've learned to listen more to my gut than my coin purse when shopping for magic.

"Tell me about that one?" I ask, pointing to it.

She grins, revealing a mouth of straight teeth and the gap between her two front ones. "Labradorite. It's a powerful one, protective knots between each sphere. It'll bring you back from Hell's gates. But you've got two of those, just with different stones."

She's pointing to my wrist, at the two strings wrapped around it.

"I think I need a third," I say, feeling the truth of the words as my mouth forms them.

"Very well." She starts to wrap it in paper, but I hold out my wrist.

"If you wouldn't mind," I say.

"Not at all."

Her fingers are cool as they graze my skin, and when I flinch, she chuckles.

"No, I ain't a vampire," she says. "Just poor circulation at my age."

I wait patiently while she ties the knots.

"I assume you know how to invoke a healing charm?" she asks.

"I do. Blood, and the intent, spoken in a word. *Heal.*"

"Good." Her eyes are assessing, traveling over my face and to my neck.

I sense the moment they focus on the scar there, and it takes all my willpower not to cover it with my hand. It ain't none of her business how I got it.

Once the beads are fastened into a bracelet, she points to the leather cord around my neck. "That your sight charm?"

"Yes'm." I pull it over my head and she loses about twenty years' age before my eyes as the sight charm's powers leave me and I see things as a normal human. Now she looks to be in her twenties, not her forties. Interesting. The witch is mixing fae glamour with whatever youth charms she uses. She's a vain creature, seems. I don't begrudge her that. If I had enough looks to pull it off, I'd be a bit vain, too.

She pulls a mortar and pestle from underneath the counter and snags a leaf of bearberry dangling from the ceiling. She places the bearberry in the mortar and spits on it, then reaches under the counter for a fine cloth bag. Might even be silk, and I long to run my fingers over it, feel its softness. I don't get to touch many fine things these days.

She takes a pinch of whatever's inside the bag and drops it into the mortar, then she grinds it up with her spittle and the bearberry. Her gaze is unfocused, likely so she can imbue the spell with her witch sight.

I look around the store while she works and spot a

board next to the door. The whole thing is darn near covered in wanted posters, so I mosey over to have a look. Some of them are old—I recognize two posters from vampires I personally staked. Any posters with yellowed edges, I tend to ignore, but for the two I already took care of, I carefully remove them from the wall.

"What are you doing over there?" the witch asks, not looking up from her task.

"I already got these vampires," I say.

"You sure?"

"They're deader than dead."

"That's how we like 'em," she says.

I'm about to respond that I share her sentiments, but the door bangs open and a mousy little man steps inside the store.

"Just a moment," the witch says, still focused on her task.

"I'm here with a new posting," the man says.

"Ah. Go ahead, then," she says.

He looks at me and sneers. "You're the charmslinger."

"None of that nasty name-calling in my shop, Gerald," the witch snaps.

"Sorry, ma'am," he says to her.

I note that he doesn't apologize to me, the one he slighted. But I'm not unaccustomed to that sort of treatment, so I give him a sarcastic smile and watch while he painstakingly tacks up a new poster. There are four faces on it instead of the usual one. All vampires. The bounty is for a nest, not an individual. My interest is already piqued.

He finished his work and turns to me. Gesturing to

the posters I hold, he says, "You can't take those with you unless you're planning to stake 'em."

"You can have 'em back," I say, holding them out like giant playing cards. "But you shouldn't put them on the board. I already killed these two."

His eyes widen. "You're the charmslinger who—"

"Gerald, I will *hex you*," the witch says.

"Sorry, ma'am," he says to her again. Then he turns back to me. "You're the bounty hunter who brought down the vamp in Lilacville?"

"That I am," I say.

"How about the pair of vampires in Halo?"

I scowl. Another bounty hunter by the name of Boone got to the pair before I could attempt it. "That wasn't my bounty," I say. "I could've done it, though."

Smirking, Gerald says, "I'm sure."

"You're welcome to join me on my next hunt." I smile as I make the offer, knowing he won't accept.

"No, thank you kindly," he says in a rush. "But maybe you should take a look at this nest in Penance." He jabs a thumb at the poster in question, then exits the shop.

"I think I will take a gander," I say to myself as the door slams shut behind him.

The thought of doing a hunt in Penance, though, does not delight me. It's the closest town to the Rift, right on the eastern edge. I don't like to go up there if I can help it. Closer you get to the Rift, the more outlaws you find, because the Rift is the tear in the earth that brought the outlaws to us. I ain't never been as close as Penance.

Also, I usually don't take town names into much account, as some are downright ridiculous—Shepherd,

Halo, Blessed, Angelwing. It's like my name, Grace. Signifies absolutely nothing about me. Pa said he named me for my ma, that she moved with grace. Well, that ain't ever been me, so it became more of a joke than anything. He finally gave up and called me Gracie, as did everyone else.

Penance is a name I can give some credence to, though. Traveling there, so close to the Rift, would be some kind of self-inflicted punishment.

"Your charm's ready," the witch says.

I untack the poster from the board and carry it over to the counter so I can take a closer look in the brighter lamplight. Penance is doing things right—an amateur would think four vampires would garner quadruple the usual bounty as a single target. But when you've got four in a nest, it's more than four times the work and four times the danger. The bounty offered is sixteen times the gold I was given for the vampire I killed tonight.

Extra oats for my horse, new boots, and some gold left over to put toward buying some land to call my home.

Four vampire faces stare up at me. Their fangs just poke below their upper lips. One has a black and pointy beard, and the vampire wearing it has a high forehead. I shudder at the mean, angry look in its eyes. The artist had to be good to get that across. *John Marlowe* reads the name beneath the picture.

One looks harmless as a sulky adolescent, couldn't have been more'n fifteen when he died. It don't have a name listed.

Another is female with a deceptively sweet face. In

the pen and ink drawing, her hair's worn in braided pigtails. Its name looks to be *Sarah Alice*.

The fourth vampire seems nearly featureless, as if the image could be a likeness of my own face, or the witch's, or Gerald's. *Leader: no picture, no name*, reads the text beneath the frame.

"You ever taken a nest?" the witch asks, peering at the poster with me. She passes me the sight charm.

"Not in recent memory." Not ever, but she doesn't need to know that. The prospect of such a large bounty is too good to ignore. I picture a little house in a valley, maybe some goats to keep Kitty company.

I put on the sight charm again. The dim store becomes immediately brighter. I nod in appreciation. The beauty of passive magic like sight and healing charms is they won't hurt my head. It's only the active magic—charms and hexes to use against someone else, for harm—that'll render a human under the weather.

"Foolish to take on a nest, but I ain't going to stop you." She huffs with impatience. "Can't give you that labradorite healing string for free, but take these."

Without waiting for my assent, she opens up a square yard of canvas and starts putting things on it—stakes, likely magicked with speed and accuracy; some tiny stones that I recognize will stop my monthly courses if I swallow one at the start; a handful of mending stones, which will heal lesser injuries and ills; and a handful of sugar cubes.

"What are those for?" I ask, pointing to the cubes.

"Your horse," she says in a tone that says she's beginning to doubt my intelligence. "Poor creature probably thought she'd get to rest easy for the night, but now you'll be riding her hard to Penance."

True enough, but Kitty never seems to mind our nonstop life. Which means the witch is right, and I ought to show her a little extra kindness.

"I'm much obliged," I say, "and so's my horse."

"Saw you ride in this afternoon. She's a beauty."

"And doesn't she know it," I say as the witch wraps up the goods and ties the bundle with a length of twine. Kitty's a buckskin, with a tan body, a dark mane and tail, dark legs, and liquid black eyes. I found her at a failing ranch, half-starved, and promptly gave the cowherd all my gold to purchase her. I've never regretted that, not once. Not even when I had to eat hardtack for two weeks until I could land my next bounty.

The witch names a price, well below what I ought to be giving her. I'd thought the witch didn't like me. Maybe she didn't and I grew on her, although that's as likely as me winning a beauty contest. More like she wants this territory rid of vampires just as much as I do.

Recalling what Gerald said about not taking the posters unless I intend to go after the bounty, I fold this one up and tuck it into the inner pocket of my duster. Then I give the witch more gold than she asked, return my hat to my head, and exit the store.

Penance is three days' ride from here, by my estimate. I haven't been there before, but I'm familiar enough with the territory's towns, especially those closer to the Rift, which I want to avoid. It should be an easy enough ride, mostly flat through the valley, with a bit of hill country, but nothing Kitty can't manage.

The street's just as quiet now as it was an hour ago, but I can sense more within it. The witch did good work on my sight charm—not just for seeing in darkness or seeing past fae glamour, but for seeing the waves of danger that waft from certain areas. I don't know, for instance, what's lurking behind a stack of firewood to the left of the brothel doors, but I know to give that area a wide berth. Could be a rattler, could be a sprite. No way to know, and no way am I going to go looking for trouble. Trouble seems to find me on its own without any help, thanks.

THREE

KITTY WASN'T THRILLED when I woke her in the stable to leave town again so quickly, but the sugar cubes softened my request and now she's loping along like she was born to travel at night. She has a sight charm of her own, woven into her bridle, that enables her to see well enough to avoid accidents when traveling through darkness. She eyes me as if I've betrayed her whenever I remove the bridle, and one of these days I'll have enough gold to hire a witch to weave a charm into her mane.

A full moon is directly overhead, meaning it's around midnight. I find a copse of trees and am pleased when the creek bed next to them still has running water despite it being early summer. Come August, this won't be the case.

Kitty's pleased about the water, too, and she gulps greedily. I toss a square of hardtack into the creek. I don't see evidence of any water fae in the area, but it doesn't hurt to show them some gratitude just the same.

I'd much rather show gratitude to a fae who isn't present than earn the ire of one who is.

Once Kitty's secure, I unfold my bedroll and settle in, risking the removal of my thigh sheath. Sleeping with stakes and a knife strapped to my leg isn't comfortable in the slightest. I keep them close by, like my holster, within arm's reach.

I'm not too terribly tired, but north of here, closer to the Rift, is a good place to travel in the day instead of at night. Better to get my rest now.

Looking up at the stars, I search for the constellations my pa taught me—constellations he learned from my ma. She died birthing me, and she was half of true American descent, making me a quarter. I have her dark hair, and Pa's blue eyes. The constellations are all I have of her stories and heritage, so I watch the passage of the wise woman with her feathered skirt as she traverses the sky. Eventually, my eyelids grow heavy, and I sleep.

My dream this night features the usual horrors—my pa held tight in the grip of a vampire. Her lips are coated in his blood. She lets him go and advances toward me.

My pa falls to the ground, dead. His neck is a smear of blood and flesh.

Kitty whickers loud enough to wake me before I have to kill my pa again in my dreams. Once in real life was bad enough. My hand flexes with the muscle memory of driving the stake into his heart, and my eyes water with their own memory of the tears I shed.

The next day passes in a haze of heat and endless prairie. We stop every now and then to let Kitty rest and nibble some grass, and I allow her to drink from any stream we come upon. Each time, I drop hardtack into the water, then nibble on a piece, myself.

We come to a house and I ask some apples from the rancher. He takes one look at my bracelets, trousers, and the scar on my neck, and he spits on the ground. "Get on out of here, charmslinger."

Two kids are playing by the well near the ranch house, close enough to have heard what their pa said to me. They spit and shout insults as Kitty and I pass, and for some reason that gives my heart a pang of sorry more than the rancher's ill reception.

Later in the afternoon, we reach another abode. The woman living there won't accept payment for the apples and bread she brings out for me, and she laughs when I offer to split wood for her. Her arms are the size of my thighs—she could probably split wood with some well-placed punches against a tree trunk.

It's such a stark difference from what I encountered earlier with the rancher and his kids, I blink rapidly and shake my head to make sure I ain't dreaming.

"I don't need your gold nor your favors," she says, bringing an extra apple to Kitty. "I can tell you're a bounty hunter, and I just hope you make this territory a safer place than it is."

I like her home, and her manner as she walks the ground. She's comfortable here. Someday, this could be me, mistress of my own little domestic life.

Too soon, it's time to continue on my journey. A grassy valley stretches before us, and Kitty and I aim ourselves at the hills on the other side. That's where we'll find Penance.

The thought of visiting a Rift town gives me the shivers. I think of turning around. The folded wanted poster in my coat burns in there like a rebuke. You don't take a poster unless you have every intention of fulfilling the bounty. I imagine the witch's reaction to me returning to her store and tacking the poster back up again. That thought alone has me urging Kitty forward.

The prairie fades behind us, opening into a desert full of scrub brush, stunted trees, and dust. White things jut up from the earth like rigid flowers, and I slow Kitty. She huffs but complies.

As we get closer, I can see even better. The white things are crosses. We're looking at a grave site.

"C'mon, girl," I say, directing her closer.

She resists, but I need to know what we're dealing with. Usually I don't find a grave site far from a town, but there's nothing else around here for a few miles yet. No church, no dusty street or false-fronted buildings.

There are trees nearby, as we're skirting along the edge of the foothills, and I see two things that answer my thoughts.

First, there's a wide creek. It'll dry up in late summer or early fall, but this grave site's proximity to running water ain't an accident. Because each of these graves is marked with not one cross, but two. The first cross to signify the religious burial. The second cross is planted about where the corpse's chest would be, with a much longer, pointier stake, to keep the body in the ground.

The dirt's fresh on top, and the grasses ain't had a chance to grow yet. A few of the graves bear bouquets— and these bouquets aren't simple collections of flowers, but rather strategic collections of herbs and ribbons, tied and knotted with magic.

I count 'em. Seventeen graves here.

Patting Kitty's neck, I say, "This here's the reason Penance is offering such a large bounty for the nest."

She dances sideways, skittish. She doesn't like it here any more than I do.

I drop some hardtack into the creek as we cross it. The water itself won't keep the vampires from returning to Penance—it's those stakes that'll keep them in the ground, and any of their reluctance to revisit the scene of their humanity after they find their sires. But the people of Penance are layering superstition upon magic, and I don't fault them for it. Seventeen graves is a massacre.

It takes us another hour to reach Penance. A sign welcomes us, proclaiming this town to be *Penance: The City of Silver*. The town glints in the sunlight, with silver details decorating the false storefronts. Silver in the shapes of crosses and protective runes is stamped into posts that hold up the shaded walkway on each side of the street. As people move about, sun reflects off of silver jewelry and buckles.

Kitty's fatigued, so my first order of business is to find a stable to let her rest and fill her belly. I pay a stable girl to give Kitty a good comb. The greedy girl asks even more than my offering. "I'll throw in some braids on her mane," she says.

I pull a tiny parcel of bone beads from one of the saddlebags and hand them to the girl. "Weave in some of these beads and it's a deal."

"Are those magical?" she asks, wrinkling her nose.

"Not if you don't want 'em to be."

Puzzling over my response, she takes the parcel from me and leads Kitty to a stall. The beads ain't magical—yet —but once I put a little blood on them and speak a couple of words, they'll give Kitty extra endurance for when we're out on the hunt.

It feels good to walk a bit on my own two feet, so I don't ask for directions to the marshal or sheriff. Exploring Penance could give me a good feel for what's been done to the people here.

A man sells "anti-vampire elixirs" from the back of a covered wagon. He's doing good business, but the only thing magic about him is how he manages not to hate himself for fleecing this town. His coin purse is growing fat on peoples' fear, and that ain't right.

A woman in the biggest wide-brimmed cowherd hat I ever saw marches over to him, fire flashing in her light gray eyes, silver hoops glinting from her earlobes. I stop to watch the spectacle as she points at him.

"You, sir, must leave Penance *at once*," she says.

"I don't see what kind of authority you have over me." He stands up to his full height. He's a whole head taller than the woman in the big hat.

"I'm the sheriff here," she says. "And you are a snake of a man, taking advantage of our town's grief to sell this false hope. I've a mind to strap you up and tie you to a pole so the vampires can get you themselves. I'll be kind enough to coat you in your own elixir. Then we can see if it works."

The elixir man shrinks in his boots and begins packing up his wagon while the crowd disperses. Some of the folks look on, anger and disappointment twisting their features.

The sheriff snaps at them, "I'm saving you the gold we can better spend on that bounty to rid Penance of the vampire nest, you fools."

And there's my opening. As the townspeople stomp off, I sidle in, friendly-like, and approach the sheriff.

"Afternoon, Sheriff."

She turns to look at me. Her hair is brown, streaked with gray, and those gray eyes are every ounce just as fiery as they were a moment before. In a cautious voice, she says, "What can I do for you, stranger?"

"I'm here on account of the bounty." I pull the poster from my coat and unfold it. As if she needs a reminder. Feeling like a fool, I fold it up again and tuck it into my coat.

"Never met a woman vampire hunter before," she says, giving me a good stare.

"Never met a woman sheriff before," I say, returning the look.

Her face cracks in a grin, and she nods. "It ain't only up to me, it's up to the folks here whether we agree to take you on."

"My experience, the town doesn't need to agree," I say. "I bring in the heads, I get paid."

"My experience, you can't bring in a nest of vampire heads without a posse." She looks up and down the street behind me. "I don't see a posse here, and I'm not giving my blessing to a hunter going out alone, woman or man."

Crossing my arms over my chest, I say, "Blessing? Are you the sheriff *and* the preacher?"

"Get a posse, stranger. Then come back and we'll talk about the nest."

Her tone leaves no room for argument, but I can be patient. More patient still, with the amount of gold being offered in the bounty. Tipping my hat at her, I take my leave and meander back up the main street.

The street's only about a half-mile long. Small alleys squeeze between the buildings, leading back to small homes that likely house the shopkeepers and their families. The far end of the street ends in a courtyard and just on the other side of that, a white church, pretty as a picture, with a modest steeple. The church is framed by the foothills on either side, nestled in there like a pea in a pod.

What sets this town apart from others are the folk—some of them men, some women—standing at the corners of each building, their eyes scanning the street and the alleys. Sheriff's smart—she posted guards. I wonder if she did that before or after they buried seventeen of their own.

I also wonder how far we are from the Rift. A day's ride? Two? I don't much like being so close.

I amble past a milliner, a general store, a blacksmith, and a saloon. Each of their signs has silver punched into them, sometimes in simple dots, sometimes in stars or crosses. Loud piano music filters through the saloon's window and I cringe. A woman should be able to enjoy her drink in a quiet place. There's a second floor to the saloon, and I'd wager that the place offers room and board as well as drink.

Sighing to myself, I square my shoulders and step through the swinging doors.

As I don't carry a vampire head in a sack this time, my entrance garners little interest from the other patrons, a group of cowherds betting their coin in a game of cards, a couple of town folk enjoying an early supper, and a painted lady with a crimson mouth who stares morosely at an empty glass.

I make my way quiet-like to the bar and take a seat on one of the stools.

"Ma'am," the bearded barkeep says.

"A whiskey, please."

His gaze goes to the scar on my neck, and then the charmed bracelets on my wrist, and then the trousers I wear. His apathetic expression twists into disapproval.

I wish I was sixteen again, with no chest to speak of, so that I could pass myself off as a man. I had two glorious years of capturing vampire bounties and enjoying the occasional glass of whiskey while nobody looked twice at my trousers. Then I grew into my curves, and no amount of cloth wrappings or baggy shirts could conceal my bosom.

I've heard some argue whether the west is a vampire's world. A man's world. A demon's world. A fae's world. I don't know which of those things is true, but I know one thing for certain: it sure as hell ain't a woman's world.

I put a gold coin on the counter and slide it across to the barkeep.

"A whiskey," I repeat.

The barkeep doesn't budge. "I don't serve charm-slingers."

"I guess I'll take my business elsewhere. Was also looking to find a place to lay my head tonight. I got plenty of gold, but that's fine. I'll look for another establishment." I move to take my gold off the counter.

"Hardin, give the charmslinger some booze," a man slurs drunkenly from one of the tables.

"I'll serve you your whiskey. We have rooms available, too." Frowning, Hardin takes the coin and fills the bottom half of a glass. It's not enough to nurse for a long spell, but I'll do my best.

Nodding at the table where someone spoke up for me —even though that speaking up included name-calling, I find my way to a shadowed corner of the room and plop down at a table. There, I watch the other patrons and think about my next steps. Last thing I want to do is gather a posse. It takes years, lifetimes even, to build trust. Besides, I tried working with a partner once and it didn't work out. Well, it didn't work out for me; it worked out fine for the lazy lout who ran off with my bounty and left me to barter passage on a ferry across the river with a demon who only just let me escape with my soul.

I could lie to the sheriff and tell her I have a posse on the way, but I've found it best not to tell tall tales to the folks I want to pay me at the end of the day. She might never find out, or she might have a charm or two on her person. Charmslingers like me aren't as uncommon as "proper" folk would like to think. Humans all over the west have been figuring out that life is just a tad easier sometimes with a little magic to help them along. They just don't like to admit as much because they think it taints them somehow. They'd rather shout slurs at the ones who use it openly. Jealous, I suppose.

That leaves me with one other option—finding a posse in name only. They stay behind, out of my way, and I pay them a set amount upon my return. Best way, really; there's no risk of betrayal. But the right person has to be a combination of greedy—wanting to take my money, vain—not wanting to mess his pretty face, and without valor—not minding that he looks like a coward for staying behind.

A man walks into the bar and takes off his hat to reveal sandy blond hair. He looks directly at me. His bright blue eyes seem to shine through the gloom, his nose is straight, his teeth all intact as he smiles.

Ladies and gents, I've found my posse.

FOUR

THE MAN STOPS at the bar, asks for two whiskeys, and once he's got 'em, he saunters back to me.

"Evening," he says.

I glance at the shuttered window. Sunlight doesn't stream through the cracks anymore. "Sure is," I say.

He nudges my nearly-empty whiskey aside with one of the fresh glasses in his hands. "I bought you a drink."

"Much obliged," I say, pushing it away from me.

He doesn't take the hint and he sits down—which is exactly what I'd hoped for, anyhow. I just can't appear too eager.

"The name's Sam Carson," he says, leaning back in his chair.

He appraises my person. His gaze lands on the scar on my neck. I let him look and give him a stare-down in return. Too handsome for hard work, although there's a faint layer of dust on his shirt and vest. Maybe he rides up and down the street, hoping to catch glimpses of his reflection in the couple of glass windows.

In a higher-pitched voice that he probably thinks sounds like me, Carson says, "Howdy, Carson, it's a pleasure to meet you. You're a good-looking fella. I'm..."

He trails off and raises his eyebrows at me expectantly, waiting for me to finish the sentence he spoke for me. I can't hide the involuntary grin that settles on my face. He's amusing enough, I'll grant him that.

"I'm a woman in search of a posse in name only," I say.

"Funny you should talk about names when you haven't told me yours."

"The name's Gracie Boswell. I'm after the nest of vampires, and Sheriff won't give me the information I need unless I have a proper group."

"I'll be in your posse, Miss Boswell," he says, dragging his chair closer to the table and leaning forward. "But I want to be in the posse in more than name. I want to help."

"You don't understand. I don't actually want help."

Eyeing the bracelets on my wrist, he says, "Miss Boswell?"

"Call me Gracie."

"Gracie." He grins again, flashing that too-pretty smile. "So you're a charmslinger?"

Funny, the way he says it, it doesn't sound like an insult.

"I am."

"Good," he says. "I don't want to work for a stupid person."

"You're not working for me," I say, internally questioning his intelligence. "You're sitting comfy-like in a saloon or your mama's kitchen while I rustle up the nest, bring in the heads, and give you a healthy portion of the bounty."

He knocks back his glass of whiskey and eyes the one he'd offered me.

"Take it," I say.

"I need a job more'n I need the whiskey," he says. "My pa kicked me out of his house. I live in Penance, but I've been staying upstairs without a home of my own."

He seems at ease in this room, and the barkeep didn't doubt he could pay when he ordered these whiskeys. His chin's smooth, meaning he shaved at some point today, but given the late hour, I'd expect more whiskers on his cheeks, which tells me he shaved late. Which likely means he slept in today.

"Your pa kicked you out for not working very hard, didn't he?" I guess.

He gapes at me, his blue eyes wide. "How'd you know? You some kind of mind-reader?"

"It ain't difficult to spot a lazy man," I say.

Carson looks like he has a retort for that, but just as he opens his mouth, someone screams outside.

Carson jumps up almost as fast as me, but I beat him to the door and rush through it, hand on my holster. It takes me a split second to calculate which charms are loaded into my gun (stunners) and reach for the thigh sheath with my other hand, where a line of stakes are fastened, point down, ready to draw.

A shadowy figure is making its way along the side of the street. It looks to have four legs and I'd think it a four-legged fae whose glamour failed, except for the fact that two of the legs are flailing behind it and struggling for purchase in the pitted dirt while the other two legs make their stubborn way forward.

Removing my gun from its holster, I send my gaze down the barrel and take careful aim. From experience, I know if I hit the abductee, the outlaw will have less resistance and will move faster. I must hit the outlaw on my first shot.

"You can't possibly see what you're doing," Carson says, disrupting my concentration.

"Don't speak," I say, lining up the shot with the outlaw and victim's progress.

Carson isn't as dumb as I thought, because he listens and shuts his yap.

I exhale, pull the trigger. Green light—too brilliant to be natural—arcs across the road and smacks right into the outlaw. The human breaks free and runs down the street toward one of the open doorways. I hurry toward the outlaw, boots pounding the street. Footsteps thud behind me but I don't spare them a glance. My focus is on one thing only: the dark lump on the side of the street.

My stake is at the ready. Might not be a vampire at all. Could be fae, who're known to take folks off and change them—or, more often, eat them. Could be a demon making good on a soul bargain. Whatever it is, a stake will at least slow them down further.

The form is still unmoving when I reach it, close enough for the toes of my boots to brush its behind. I kick it over. It has the face of a demon, but it's a vampire. The eyes are full of the hatred and fury of a cornered animal. The cruel face is pale, fangs puncturing its own lips in a grimace so twisted, my heart stops. I could be looking into the face of my pa all over again.

"Gracie," Carson says. He's holding a stake of his own and nudging his elbow into mine.

I don't move.

"Gracie, its hand is moving. The charm's wearing off."

I try to shake off my stupor. Going still as a scared coyote at the sound of a gunshot is not my usual reaction to seeing a vampire's face. I heft the stake in my hand.

Carson lunges toward the outlaw.

"Wait," I say.

But his momentum keeps him going. He can't stop. He jabs his stake into the vampire's chest before I can move to hold him back.

The vampire's body bows forward, its fingers curling into talons, and the fury leaves its eyes.

"Dammit, Carson," I say, removing the stake. But it's too late—the vampire has met its second death.

"What'd I do?" Carson holds his hands out.

I shove the blood-blackened stake into his grasp. He visibly flinches before wiping the wood against the ground.

"I could've questioned it." Likely, it wouldn't have answered me with anything except lies, but lies can tell their own sort of truth when you know what you're looking for.

I could try to rustle up a witch or someone else with a necromancy spell, but it would probably be a wasted and expensive effort. It might rise on its own tomorrow night, but I don't aim to stick around that long. Better to just let this one go.

The sheriff runs up, her hair in a braid, her hat gone. I bet she was just sitting down to a nice supper after a long day, and for a brief moment I'm envious of the idea of a quiet, domestic life.

"What am I looking at?" she asks. It's less a question, more a demand. I can appreciate that.

"You're looking at the bounty hunter who's on the case of the nest terrorizing Penance," I say.

"And her posse," Carson adds, pointing his thumb at his chest.

Sheriff shakes her head. "You can't have a posse of one or two."

"That's why there are three of us." A man steps from the alley nearest us.

I nearly fling my stake at his chest, but he holds his hands up and smiles—not a smile of friendship, but a smile to show he don't have fangs. He's got a brutish look —this here's a man who's been in a tussle or two. His nose has been broken, but he's got all his teeth. He stands taller than anyone here, possibly taller than anyone I've ever seen. He, too, wears a sheath with stakes around his thigh. He's a vampire bounty hunter, like me.

He ain't pretty like Carson, but even in the dim moonlight I can see he has gorgeous, light brown eyes.

If I'm needing someone else on my posse—in name only, of course—I suppose he won't hurt. As long as he and Carson stay back and let me do my work, they can't double-cross me.

Nodding, Sheriff says, "I suppose that'll do. I'd feel

better if there were seventy of you, but beggars can't be choosers. We need our spare folk for the town militia."

Nestled next to the stakes on my thigh sheath is a blade magicked wicked sharp. I start working on the vampire's neck. Carson looks away, a sickened expression on his face. Yep, he'll be staying behind while I hunt the nest, no doubt about it.

"I know this bloodsucker ain't on the wanted poster," Sheriff says. "Why're you taking off the head?"

"You have a name, Sheriff?" I ask.

"Sheriff works just fine," she says.

"Well, Sheriff, the vampire's dead, but I don't stop at the staking. Demons can manipulate the dead, fae can work glamour on 'em, and I once met a witch in Halo selling necromancy spells from the back of her covered wagon. But you slice off the head, ain't nothing can bring a person or an outlaw back."

The new brute looks impressed, but Carson still wears a faintly sickened grimace.

Once the head is severed, I grip it by the hair and shove it at Carson. To his credit, he takes it without vomiting.

"Get rid of that," I say.

"Maybe this other guy should get rid of it," he suggests, holding out the head.

"I gave you that job," I say.

He frowns, but says, "Fine."

To the sheriff, I say, "I'll be staying in town tonight. Tomorrow, you and anyone with notions of where I should start looking for the nest will enjoy a conversation with me at the saloon."

"Fair enough," she says. "I see you proved yourself."

I don't tell her that it was Carson who staked the vampire, and another point goes to his favor when he doesn't say so, either.

The new brute folds his arms over his chest as if he's waiting some instruction, too.

"I'll see you in the saloon tomorrow, as well," I tell him. Then I turn on my boot heel and march back to the saloon, hoping the barkeep will give me a quiet room far from that tonking piano music I can, even now, hear in the corners of my mind. Slinging one charm won't give me a massive headache, but it ain't a comfortable feeling, either.

FIVE

AS SOON AS I WAKE, I do a quick sweep of the room to make sure all my belongings are where they ought to be. The saddlebag with my charms is under my pillow. My gold bag is in my hand. The sack with my spare change of clothes is draped next to the door and I'll hire out someone to wash it for me while I'm downstairs meeting with Sheriff. My boots are right next to the bed.

Dawn light slants across the hardwood floor. No carpet in here. Lucky for me, it won't get cold until October. By then I'll be long gone, my bags weighed down by the bounty. I want to be far from this place before the days get too short. Summer's when humans have the slightest advantage—more light means less time for the bloodsuckers to hunt.

I make my way to the little washstand next to the window. After splashing some water on my face, I peer outside. My room faces the street, which is quiet at this hour, no one but a lone cowherd riding along on a weary-looking horse.

Carvings etched into the window ledge catch my eye. They're crosses, looped together with a pattern of twisting vines. I trace them with my finger. They're an old superstition from a decade back. We used to think symbols of the cross would protect us from all manner of the outlaws. Engravers and carpenters, leatherworkers and jewelers, embroiderers and seamstresses all did booming business for a stretch as demand for spiritual symbols on every good imaginable shot up to heaven's gates.

Turns out, ain't much can save us from the outlaws. Not garlic, not holy water, not crosses—unless the ends of those crosses are sharpened into stakes. Magic can save us from the outlaws—we have to use the outlaws' own tools against them.

And in a steamy cow pie of irony, there's still a lot of humans who refuse to touch the magic.

I dress in a fresh shirt and underclothes, put on my dirty trousers and boots, and head downstairs in the hopes of breaking my fast.

The barkeep is nowhere to be seen, but a blond-haired woman stands behind the counter, loading a cast-iron pan of scrambled eggs onto a platter. "I'm Margaret Hardin," she says. "Wife of the barkeep."

"Pleased to meet you, Mrs. Hardin. I'm Gracie Boswell," I say, giving a longing glance to the pile of eggs.

"Help yourself," she says. "It's only you and two others here, and they stayed up late pissing away their gold in a card game with my low-life spouse. My husband is still asleep, the oaf."

"Who came out ahead?" I ask, more to make conversation than satisfy any curiosity. I settle into one of the stools at the bar.

"The big 'un. Man they call Levi Boone."

I nearly fall off my stool. Levi Boone? I've heard of him—he's another bounty hunter and he's beat me to more than one take. The pair of bloodsuckers in Halo, for example. I traveled all the way there only to find he'd already killed the vampires deader than dead and made off with the gold.

It wasn't just that nest, either. The man has been a blight on my goals, reaching more'n one bounty just as I raced into town.

And here he was again. Well, I'd gotten here first, and Sheriff said the job was mine. Levi Boone can go take himself to the Rift if he thinks he'll get in on my hunt.

Mrs. Hardin looks under the counter for some cutlery, which she places on the bar top. She hasn't noticed my shock. "He's a genial fellow. I knew a man like him when I was a young, young girl. Same name, too, I think. Levi. It's common enough, I s'pose. You know that feeling, when you feel like you've met someone before?"

I nod noncommittally, not too keen on chatter. All I can think about is beating Levi Boone to the bounty.

"It's a comfort, but also a mite eerie," she says. "I meet someone every now and then and I wonder if I knew them in a past life. It ain't very Christian of me, but I think about reincarnation at times."

Letting her talk wash over me, I take one of the empty plates from the bar and load some eggs onto it, along with a piece of blackened toast and a generous scoop of berry preserves.

"Will you be needing anything else?" she asks.

"Coffee, please, if you have it."

"I do," she says, turning to go through a doorway behind the bar.

As I'm the only soul in the saloon, and the player piano is thankfully not playing, I settle in at the bar and dig in to my meal. It's cheerful in here, and coffee's coming, and I'll meet with the sheriff and the giant man to talk over details of my upcoming vampire hunt. Only thing that would make it more cheerful is if Kitty were nearby with a big trough of sweet hay and a contented look in her big black eyes.

Wait a minute. That giant man. Mrs. Hardin called Levi Boone "the big 'un." I couldn't have accepted Levi Boone as a member of my posse, could I have?

I'd say fate ain't that cruel, but the scar on my neck proves fate *is* cruel.

A shadow falls across my plate and I look up to see the owner of said shadow. It's the brute from last night. His skin is darkly tanned, his eyes a light caramel. He has a strong, square chin, freshly shaved, and a head full of short-cropped, black hair. The sun shifts around him in some kind of trick and I have to squint harder for a moment before the light rights itself. I'd suspect glamour was at play, but my sight charm is strong and would help me see through it.

He holds out a hand. "Levi Boone."

Rift take me now.

I set down my forkful of steaming eggs and reluctantly shake his hand. His grip is firm, and his palm dwarfs mine. I'm no delicate maiden, but this man could crunch my hand the same way I could crumple a piece of parchment.

"Gracie Boswell," I say.

"I've heard of you," he says, his lips twitching in an almost smile.

Fighting the scowl that desperately wants to make an appearance on my visage, I say, "I've heard of you, too. I take it you're not from around these parts, either?"

"No, ma'am," he says. "I make my current home in the mountain territory up north of here."

"What do you think of the valley and plains?" I ask. What I really want to know is what he thinks of scooping bounties out from under me every few months.

"It's dry," he says. "I'm thirsty all the time. And when I face away from the mountains, the landscape plays tricks on my eyeballs—I keep making out hills where there ain't nothing."

I've never been past the Rift to the northern territory, but someday I'd like to go, see the towering land masses everyone talks about. I wonder what Kitty would think of them, or if she'd even notice. Her focus always seems to be on the here and now. Is there sturdy ground beneath her feet, and hay in her bucket? If so, all's right in the world.

"I imagine you're going to head out today, early as possible?" he asks.

Wouldn't he like to know. He'll probably plan to leave an hour in advance.

"Yep," I say slowly. "Are you really interested in being a part of *my* posse? Not going it alone?"

"I am," he says.

"And you want to tell me why you ain't going off to take down these vampires on your own?"

He smiles, slow and easy. "It's a nest of vampires. I'd have to be damn stupid to try for it on my own."

I hear the mocking censure in his tone. He knows I'd rather do this job without a posse, and he's trying to piss me off.

He's succeeding.

"It's only stupid if it can't be done," I say flatly, refusing to give him the satisfaction of an emotional reaction. "You and the cowherd'll come out partway with me, then sit tight somewhere safe. Once I'm done, I'll bring in the heads and meet you at an agreed-upon locale where I'll divvy up the bounty with the two of you."

He frowns. "That ain't how a posse works."

"I'm redefining the term." I take a bite of eggs, swallow.

The barkeep's missus comes out with a large cup of coffee and sets it down before me. Her neck stretches so she can look up at the giant sitting at my side. "Coffee for you, Mister Boone?"

"No, thank you, ma'am," he says in a deep rumble. "These eggs and toast'll suit me just fine. Did you cook all this yourself?"

"Well, there's my boy back there. He helps me, fetches whatever I need."

"Sounds like a good lad," Boone says.

She smiles. "He is. Loves getting into mischief, though."

"Aw, that's natural enough. I got into a fair bit of mischief as a boy, too. I hope I turned out all right in the end."

"Oh, you seem to have done just fine for yourself," Mrs. Hardin says.

Boone flashes a smile at her, his white teeth flashing against his dark skin and his caramel eyes twinkling.

Well, aren't the two of them set up to be lifelong friends. I take another bite of my toast and watch their interaction from the corner of my eye.

Mrs. Hardin beams at him and fairly bats her eyelashes. "I've some bacon coming off the griddle, too."

"That sounds mighty tasty, thank you kindly," he says.

I wait until she bustles back to the kitchen again and then I look at Boone. "You always make friends so easy?"

"It don't cost nothing to be friendly," he says, then shovels a forkful of eggs into his mouth.

Friendliness can cost a lot, but one thing I've learned in my twenty-four years is that it's better to save your breath than try to convince someone with an opposing philosophy that your philosophy is the right one. Besides, friendliness has different costs and rewards depending on your gender.

"You seen Carson around this morning?" I ask.

He snorts. "He was still snoring in the room next to mine when I came down."

That settles it. I don't have any use for layabouts on this hunt. Carson'll stay back, and Boone'll babysit.

I smear a giant dollop of berry preserves on my toast and take a bite. Sweetness explodes over my tongue and I close my eyes. Between the breakfast and the coffee, I am completely spoiled. Town life don't seem so bad when it presents me with these kinds of luxuries.

Boone sets down his fork. "You smell that?"

"The bacon?" I ask. Because it smells mighty good.

"No. Smoke."

Immediately I look to the doorway leading to the kitchen, but there's no sign of smoke there. No scent of it, either.

"I don't smell anything, Boone."

"Bacon's covering it up." He jumps up and rushes to the saloon doors.

I follow him to the boardwalk. There're more people around now, slowly making their way into shops, trying to get their errands run before the sun climbs too high up in the sky.

Boone looks right and left, then stops and stares. I follow his gaze to the north end of the street, where the little church is nestled within the foothills. The courtyard in front of it is empty this early in the day, and nobody's paying the church any mind.

Nobody except me and Boone sees the lick of flames along the north side.

SIX

"FIRE!" Boone shouts, pointing.

As I watch, the flames spread along the wall, orange and yellow tongues, hungry as a demon after a person's soul. My heart races like a frightened colt's because there is no doubt in my mind this fire is no accident.

When a vampire knows a town is coming after it, the first place it goes for revenge is the church. That's why the vampire in Shepherd went after the preacher's daughter. From what I can discern, the vampires are aiming to destroy hope with such antics. Attacks on churches go to the heart of these little towns.

Just like my stakes will go to the hearts of the vampires that perpetrate these acts.

Someone screams, and people run out of the shops. Men and women either climb on horses or start running for the church, grabbing buckets as they go. Several people rush past me, jostling me, then I find my feet and I'm running, too.

I spot Boone ahead, already on his way. "Boone! Where's the nearest stream?"

He shouts over his shoulder, "Just behind the church!"

I run, along with several others. Someone has an extra bucket and hands it to me. We line up from the stream to the church, passing buckets filled with water. Smoke billows all around us, and the crackle of flames fills my ears. My world narrows to the act of taking a bucket from the man next to me and passing it to the woman on my other side. Nobody speaks. There ain't nothing to say.

When the people closest to the fire get tired out or overheated, they move to the other end of the line. I mentally catalogue my spells. Nothing I have is any use against a structure fire. I look around as I pass water buckets, seeking out a witch. Just as I spy her, a feeling of energy and strength comes over me. She's chanting and lining up stones in the dirt, transferring energy to the people in the line. Her magic won't put out the fire, either, but she can help us fight it.

The same people who would scorn me for being a charmslinger don't hesitate a second about accepting the witch's help now.

An hour later, the flames are nearly out, and the eastern side of the little church is a smoldering ruin. All the townsfolk are covered in soot and sweat. My throat's parched, but I barely have the energy to stand, much less lift a drink of water to my lips.

This ain't ideal conditions for hunting vampires,

what with my body's aches, pains, and thirst, but putting off the hunt isn't doing this town any favors, either.

I spy Carson and Boone in the crowd of people heading back up the main street. They must feel my gaze on them because they turn as one and stop to wait for me.

"Where do you two want to hunker down while I hunt?" I ask when I reach them. "I aim to get information from Sheriff within the hour and set out, so I expect you to do the same. It would be good if we could pick a direction that's convenient for us all."

Carson shakes his head. "I'm not in this to be a coward."

"Could've fooled me last night," I say. "You didn't even want to touch the blood."

"At least I didn't freeze up and forget to stake the vampire," he retorts.

Boone raises his hands. "Enough. This ain't no way to work together."

"That's not a problem," I say, glaring at Carson, "because he ain't working with me."

Cursing, Carson turns around and walks away.

I throw a hand up after him and look at Boone. "See? He's like a little child. I don't want to work with someone like that."

"You don't want to work with anyone," Boone says, raising a single dark eyebrow.

"Ain't that the truth." I look up at the remains of the church. Nobody asked how the fire started, but it was very likely a vampire from the nest, trying to widen his foothold in Penance.

"I got a hunch about something," I say to Boone.

"Is your hunch telling you that you have to accept my help as part of a *real* posse? Because that's what my hunch is saying."

Shaking my head, I march around the blackened portion of the church and begin looking for footprints. It's easy enough to find them in the now muddy ground, but those aren't the ones I'm interested in.

Probably I wouldn't see them if it weren't for my sight charm, but faint tracks lead from the church and up toward the foothills behind it. I squat down and point at one of the marks. Boone comes over to peer at it.

"You're thinking this was arson," he says.

"I am." I sigh. There ain't nowhere for a vampire to hide nearby. Certainly not in the church, not when it set fire to the place.

He's quiet for a spell, staring at the footprint. "Demon or vampire?"

"Not sure. But given the nest I'm about to start hunting..."

"Vampire," he finishes.

"Yep. But could it have started the fire and had enough time to hightail it out of here before the sun rose? Let's go talk to the sheriff." I stand up and dust the dirt from my hands. Blisters have formed on my palms from passing pails to put out the fire. I frown at the sting, then march forward.

"Don't you have a charm for your hands?" Boone asks.

"Not going to waste it on something like blisters."

Reaching into his pocket, he pulls out a tiny parcel wrapped in waxed paper. Opening it up, he shows me a polished stone, blotchy brown and red. Jasper, looks like. "Hold this for a moment. It's already invoked."

I stare at him. "You're a charmslinger, too?"

"If the name fits, I s'pose so." He shrugs those massive shoulders and holds up the stone. "You want this or not?"

"What about you?" I ask. "Don't you want to save it for something more important? I already have my own mending stones."

"The leader of this posse should have full use of her hands," he says simply. "I want you to have it."

I take it from him, not wanting to be ungracious, and also a mite curious about what kind of power it holds. Soothing coolness flows over my palms as soon as my skin makes contact with the stone. I can't hold in my exhale of relief, then I flick a glance at Boone, feeling embarrassed. "It's good magic. Who made this charm?"

"A witch in Halo."

"She still around?"

"I've no idea."

I nod and we walk to the saloon. The sheriff's standing outside, holding a plate of what looks to be my eggs and toast with jam. I narrow my eyes at her and she shrugs. "I only had a bite. The eggs are cold, but I'm hungry. Mrs. Hardin was going to throw it out seeing as how it's nearly dinner, but I didn't want you to lose it if you wanted it."

"I'm much obliged," I say.

"Where's mine?" Boone asks.

"She already replaced it with a luncheon."

I raise my eyebrows at him. I don't know how he inspired such admiration after their short meeting, but maybe there's something to his idea of friendliness after all.

Besides, being friendly ain't the same as being a friend.

Boone hurries inside to his plate.

"I'm down to just Boone in the posse," I tell the sheriff, "but I don't want to wait any longer. Fairly certain it was a vamp set fire to the church."

"You saw the prints, too?"

"Yep. So I'd like to get out there sooner rather than later. Guessing the vampire what started the fire didn't get far before needing to take shelter. Not sure how it got away at all. You have caves around the church?"

"Not here, no. Barely any shade from trees, as you can see. Beats me how he did it." Shaking her head, she says, "But with a posse of two, you're going to take on a vampire nest? I don't think this is wise. Three was bad enough. Two's even worse."

I flick my glance toward Boone. "He's surely got to count as at least two people on his own. Possibly three."

She doesn't smile, but the corners of her eyes lift up. "I like your humor. I hope you don't die out there."

"I share those hopes."

"Foothills are your best bet," she says. "You still have that wanted poster on you?"

"I do." I pull it from my coat and flatten it out on the bar. The four faces look up at me. The unnamed adolescent; John Marlowe, the vampire with mean eyes and a pointy-beard; the sweet-faced female vampire, Sarah Alice; and the featureless, unnamed leader.

"Hardin, you have ink and a quill?" Sheriff hollers.

The barkeep comes in from the back room, bearing both. Looking tired as anything, probably from that night playing poker with Boone and Carson, he sets the items down on the bar. He must've been doing some writing on his own, because his fingers are blackened with ink.

Sheriff's handwriting is awful, but she sketches out a rough map of the area. "Terrain up this way, east of us, gets especially rocky. There are caverns kids used to get lost in before the Rift. After the Rift opened, mamas didn't let their kids go exploring."

Smart mamas. The Rift tore a hole in the earth and out from it poured every preternatural creature from humanity's nightmares.

She draws another line through the mountains. "The Rift goes through hereabouts, which you probably already know."

"I do," I say, although I was tryin' to forget. It doesn't sit well with me to be this close to it.

"So that's my best bet on where you can find the nest. But there's this area up over here." She circles a blank section of her "map" and jabs the quill at it so hard that the ink splotches. "Rocks aplenty, and at least one cave."

Boone examines the map and rests his giant thumb on another blank area. "Has anyone poked around this region?"

"There's nothing there," Sheriff says, frowning at it. "Just an old well. I doubt a nest of vampires is huddling inside a well."

Boone looks troubled. "There's no house?"

"Not for about thirty years," she says. "It burned down shortly after the Rift."

"We'll try that first rocky area in the foothills," I say, standing up and reaching for the paper.

The sheriff shakes my hand and her eyes are serious as she says, "I stopped praying after the Rift, but I'm going to start again in the hopes of your success. Don't die out there."

"Thank you kindly, Sheriff," I say.

She shakes Boone's hand as well before leaving the saloon. Nobody else is around, although I can hear the missus in the back kitchen, humming the melody of a blood ballad, one of the sorrowful songs written after the Rift that tell of the ensuing tragedies.

I swivel on my seat to face Boone squarely, eye to eye. "It would be best if you'd give up on this posse idea," I say. "I'd be mighty grateful if you'd back the hell off."

He smiles, shakes his head. "Not a chance. We're bringing down the nest, and we're doing it together."

"I don't see why you don't just do it on your own, seein' as how you're so capable," I grumble.

"I have a gut feeling this'll be a bigger job than usual," he says, "and I listen to my gut. What do you say, Boswell?"

He holds out his right hand, daring me with his caramel gaze to shake. I know that once I do, it's as good as a contract with a demon. Irreversible, indisputable.

"And if I don't agree with you?" I ask. "What if I take off while you're not looking?"

"I go straight to the sheriff and we haul you back from the hills."

Squinting at him, I try to gauge his sincerity. His eyes

never leave my face, his hand never wavers. Rift take me, I'm going to do this.

I hold out my hand and take his. We're a posse now, me and Levi Boone.

I hope I don't regret this, but I've no doubt I will.

SEVEN

BOONE STANDS UP. "I'll gather food, charms. What do you need?"

I list off a few things, including hardtack—which is as much for me as any water fae we might need to appease, extra stakes because it never hurts to have more on hand, and some oats for the horses.

"That's it?" he asks.

"I stocked up before coming to Penance," I say. "You think you can finish the shopping in an hour?"

He nods and opens his mouth to say something when the sheriff bursts back into the saloon doors, a weeping woman at her side.

The woman's red hair is streaked with silver strands, and her heart-shaped face is pale with shock. Several rings of silver cover her fingers, but that's her only adornment.

"The vampires," she says in a sob. "They took them."

"Calm down, Minerva," she says, "and tell the posse what you told me."

"My babies," the woman says. "All of my babies."

"The vampires took your *babies*?" I ask in horror.

"Minerva Browning's youngest is not yet twenty-one," Sheriff says, not unkindly. She squeezes the woman's shoulder in comfort. "The vampires took the youngest, Jacob."

"My Jakey," Mrs. Browning says. "We woke up and he was gone."

"Are you certain it was vampires?" I find myself touching the scar on my neck, and I force my hand away from it.

"Yes. I saw the fangs. I cut one with my kitchen knife, and it bled black." She starts to say more, but breaks down into tears.

Sheriff finishes for her, "She has two other sons, and a daughter. All three of them rode out early this morning to search for Jacob. We're fearing the worst if they come upon the nest."

"Do they use charms?" I ask.

Mrs. Browning pulls herself up and glares so hard, I'd think she was a demon trying to hypnotize me with her gaze. "We are a *respectable* family," she hisses. "Unlike *you*, charmslinger."

Which don't answer my question, but if her offspring do use charms, they certainly haven't shared that fact with her. I'll have to go into the rescue on the assumption they're without ample defense.

"Hey, now, none of that name-calling," Sheriff says.

Boone steps in between me and the woman. "You might not want to verbally attack the people who are going to bring back your children."

Mrs. Browning's shoulders fall again. "Bring them... bring them back?"

"That's the goal," I say from around Boone's massive shoulder. "I can't make no promises, given we don't have much information, but we're going to try."

Mrs. Browning doesn't look at me; she only has eyes for Boone. "Thank you," she whispers, and her eyes fill with tears once more.

Sheriff leads her away, arm wrapped around the woman's bony shoulders.

Once they're out of sight, I flick Boone's bicep. "I don't need any rescuing."

"Sure you don't," he says. "Minerva Browning looked quite ready to tear you apart with her bare hands, easy as she'd pluck a hen."

"I can protect myself," I say, marching to the saloon doors and stepping through them. Over my shoulder, I say, "Our timeline's been shortened if we aim to find any of her children alive. We leave in a quarter hour. You need a horse?"

"I have one at the stable yonder." He exits the saloon and points to the same establishment where I stabled Kitty. "Name of Pegasus."

"I'll bring yours around with mine and meet you here," I say, then head off without a second glance at him.

———

BOONE'S MOUNT is a sturdy mare with a coat the color of dusted sunshine. I half expected her to buckle under his weight when he first climbed into her saddle, but both horse and rider appear quite comfortable as we ride up into the foothills beyond the church. We're able to follow a trail left by what we assume to be Minerva Browning's children on their own horses, until Boone issues a quiet, "Wait."

He and Pegasus come to a halt, so Kitty and I do as well. The hairs on the back of my neck prickle with unease. My sight charm isn't doing much for me right now, because all that I can see around us are stunted trees, gray and tan boulders, and grasses jutting up from the rocky earth.

"Someone's coming," Boone whispers.

I don't know how he can tell, but then I feel the vibrations coming up from the ground and I hear the pounding hoofbeats.

Over the crest of one of the hills come three saddled horses, their eyes wide with fright, their reins flowing freely behind them as they flee an unknown terror. Their riders are nowhere to be seen.

"Head them off," I say, nudging Kitty forward. "Yah!"

She bursts into speed, hooves thudding against the ground. Boone does the same with Pegasus, and now I see where his horse gets her name—she seems to fly across the landscape, so fast it doesn't look like she's touching earth.

Boone and Pegasus pull ahead and around the fleeing horses. The frightened beasts look as if they'll plow right into Boone and Pegasus, but Boone rides with them for a bit, slowing Pegasus little by little. Kitty and I catch up, and we slow down, too, showing the panicked horses that there's nothing to fear.

Eventually, we get them to slow to a jog, and then stop altogether. Their coats are wet and salty as they've been running in the midafternoon sun. They need water, so I jerk my head toward a nearby stream and Boone nods. We herd them over, where they drink. I pull a piece of hardtack from one of my bags and drop it in the stream. It's not much more than a trickle of water, but it don't hurt to show respect.

A smear of red decorates one of the other horses' saddles.

"Boone," I whisper, so as not to startle them.

He nods.

"The Brownings can't have gotten far," I say. It means we'll catch up with them sooner rather than later.

I hope they're alive when we find them.

Boone reaches out and runs a hand over a horse's neck, steady and calm. Then he turns Pegasus around and starts toward Penance. The horses follow his lead, and once he has them at a good gallop, he pulls back. This time, they keep going. They know where home is, and comfort.

Which is more'n I can say for myself.

———

WE MAKE our way up and over the low ridge of hills surrounding the church. Before us are mountains and more hills to the west and north, where the Rift crosses, and prairie and desert southwest. Rocky foothills lie to the southeast, holding those caves Sheriff mentioned. The caves are our best bet. As we move in that direction,

I keep my eyes wide open for signs of tracks or anything the Browning siblings might have left behind as a clue.

"North or south?" Boone asks, following my darting gaze.

"We should split up," I say. "You take one direction, I take the other. Fastest way to find the vampires and those kids."

Seems strange to call them kids when they're all around my age. But they're Minerva Browning's children, and the fact they have a mother makes them seem younger for some reason.

"We ain't splitting up," Boone says.

I don't know what comes over me, but the ferocity in his voice and the line of his jaw has me staring. His face is smooth-shaved and I'm surprised I haven't taken a moment to appreciate it before now.

While I gaze at him like a lovesick antelope, he continues, "Splitting up is madness. What are you trying to do, get us both killed?"

"No," I say, finally snapping out of my reverie. "I'm trying to perform a rescue. Seems to me you'd be jumping at the fifty-fifty chance of finding the nest on your own and claiming the bounty." It still smarts that he's beat me to several bounties over the years.

"I ain't in this for the bounty," he mutters.

My ears prick up at that. "Really. So you'd let me keep your share?"

"Never said that." A faint smile graces his smooth face.

Yeah, I thought as much. I don't much feel like

arguing about us parting ways, because I know my method is the faster one. Safer, not so much. But faster.

So I wait until he and Pegasus are trailing behind a ways while he lets her nibble a bit of grass so he can look for signs of travel in the dirt. I lean forward on Kitty and gently squeeze my calves against her sides. She shoots forward like a charm from my pistol.

"Hey!" Boone shouts. "Where are you—dammit—"

I know Pegasus is fast, but Kitty and I have a good lead, and if we run hard for a while, like she wants to do, we can shake him entirely. As Kitty gallops, I keep my eyes open, alert for any sign of the missing kids.

"Boswell!" Boone shouts.

I risk a glance over my shoulder. He's far behind. Kitty and I are well on our way to freedom.

Then he holds up a leather bag and smiles.

It's one of my bags—and when I look at the buckles on either side of Kitty's saddle, I realize it's the bag with my extra charms.

I consider letting him keep the bag while I go off to find a nest of vampires armed with only the six charms in my pistol and the stakes fastened to my thigh sheath.

But that would be total madness, and I'm only partly mad.

And we shook on our partnership, blast everything to hell. I shouldn't have tried to take off to begin with.

"Damn you to the Rift, Levi Boone!" I shout, slowing Kitty and turning her around.

How did he get my saddlebag? I examine the buckles on the saddle. The leather and hardware's intact. At some point, he unbuckled the bag and tugged it away without me even noticing. That shouldn't be possible.

He used a charm, that has to be it. Something for stealth, or distraction. Maybe when I was admiring his strong, shaved jaw a few moments ago, he was busy tugging loose my saddlebag.

I never felt like such a fool as I do now.

He still holds the bag aloft, like it's some kind of reward and he's waiting for a photographer to record his likeness.

Face burning with humiliation, I ride up next to him and yank the bag from his grasp. His chuckle is almost too deep for my ears.

"Let's you and me stick together, all right, Boswell?" he says while I studiously ignore him and try to fasten the buckles of the saddlebag.

I shrug as if it don't matter to me one way or the other, which is a wordless lie given the fact I was just urging my horse to run like our lives depended on it.

"Fine," I say. "North or south?"

"South," he says.

"Pretty country that way." We aim our horses and head up into the foothills.

"Yeah?" he asks. "How do you know about it?"

"It's the way I came in to Penance."

"What were you doing down that direction?" he asks.

"Making a vampire deader than dead in Shepherd."

He nods as we ride. "And before that?"

"Making other vampires deader than dead in other towns." *When you didn't beat me to the bounties*, I think, but I don't say that part out loud. I urge Kitty to pick up some speed and hope Boone gets the hint that I'm not particularly interested in shooting the breeze.

Either he's oblivious to the hint, or he doesn't much care for my hint, because he urges Pegasus to keep pace and he asks, "So is that all you do? Make vampires deader than dead?"

"For the most part." Our surroundings are stunted bushes and dust. In the distance, the foothills guarding the mountains that enclose the Rift. Behind us, a river and surrounding plains. It's pretty, in its way. It'd be a mite prettier if I could enjoy it in quiet.

"Where do you call home?" he asks.

I huff in frustration. "Why do you keep asking so many questions?"

"Just curious, is all." He's quiet a moment and I hope he'll drop it. Then he says, "Where's home for you?"

"Nowhere."

He's quiet then, and I risk a peek over at his face. He ain't looking at me, but at the prairie farther south that grows along the river. It's all flowing grasses that ripple in the breeze. I had a dog when I was a girl, name of Sparks, and he had fur that same gold and tan color. I'd run my hand over his fur and it would bend down like the grasses of the prairie.

I miss that dumb dog sometimes. He went and got himself killed. He knew he wasn't supposed to go to the creek without me or Pa to throw some bread or berries in. I cried for Sparks a whole week before my sadness turned into anger, and then I honed it into a determination to not let it happen again.

Kitty's the first creature I've allowed myself to love

since then, and I already cry sometimes when I think about the possibility of her dying before me.

Then I remember the work I do for my living, and I think Kitty dying first ain't too likely. Kitty's gonna outlive me, and I just know whoever takes her in will be as charmed by her beauty and kind demeanor as I've been.

Once we get farther into the foothills, the grasses have shortened to nothing and all I can see is scrub brush and dirt. The rocky terrain reveals large, tan boulders and hollows that could lead to caverns or simply shadows. This far past midday, the vampires will be hiding. Boone and I tie up the horses and hike around, stakes held aloft. We take turns peering into the darkness between boulders, finding more than one little hollow. Sheriff's right, there are plenty of caves up here. None look big enough to hide a nest during the day, but maybe we just haven't found the right place yet.

We take turns sneaking toward shadowy entrances, peeking in, the toes of our boots poised on the edge of the sinister dark.

"You have a good sight charm?" I ask Boone.

"Good enough," he says.

I think of testing him on that, but if he says he can see into those tiny crevices and into the caverns of nothing, I'll have to trust him. I have to trust him on something, or we'll be doing this forever.

For the first time, I'm very nearly grateful I'm not alone.

EIGHT

THE SUN IS SINKING below the foothills, shadows stretching longer. Boone seems to realize this the same time I do, and we scurry across boulders and rock faces to return to our horses.

"We'll be safest if we spend the night out on the prairie," he says.

Which I know, of course. If I weren't panting for breath from our race down the rocks, I'd ask him how big of a fool he thinks I am. But I need my breath. I don't know how he can move so fast. Some kind of charm, probably. He's not even breathing hard. I make a note to ask him about it when my lungs are capable of producing enough air for speech.

We reach the horses and I'm gripping my side. Kitty and Pegasus are pawing the dusty earth beneath their hooves, ears flicking this way and that in a show of nerves. Boone and I free their reins from the tree stump we tethered them to, then we're in the saddles and encouraging them to go as fast as they want. We need to get as far out in the open as possible, which will give the vampires less time to find us when they emerge from wherever they're hiding.

Because no doubt in my mind, Boone and I aren't the only hunters out here.

We find a place where the grass is a little greener, and sure enough, there's a trickling stream, probably an offshoot of the river. I drop in a piece of hardtack.

Boone squints at me. "What's that for? There can't be a fae in this tiny amount of water."

I shrug. Maybe I'm superstitious. Maybe it's too much to both remove the heads of vampires *and* burn them. Maybe sleeping with my hand on the butt of my gun is going to get me accidentally charmed with something nasty someday. But it's kept me alive this long.

Not far from the trickle of water is the foundation of a long-collapsed home. I use my boot to shove aside a porcelain washtub, curious if we can use it for washing our grimy faces, but there's a huge crack down the middle, gaping like a mocking smile.

There's nothing else useful in the rubble. I imagine the place has been looted for valuables a thousand times over the past thirty years.

"What d'you think happened to them?" I ask Boone.

He looks over from where he's combing down Pegasus. "To who?"

"To the people who lived here before. You think they died after the Rift? Or that their homestead failed before that?" I should give Kitty a brush-down, too, so I leave the old home's remains and make my way to my horse.

"No idea." His hands are sure as he combs Pegasus's

coat. The mare practically rolls her eyes in pleasure at his touch.

Trying to focus on anything except Boone's movements and big hands, I say, "I like to think they got away right before the Rift. Traveled back east to visit relatives on the railroad, bringing all kinds of wondrous tales of their adventures, and maybe a nugget of silver or gold they found in a shallow river bed when they stopped for a rest during the journey. They just reached right down and plucked a shiny rock out of the water."

I stop brushing Kitty and look over at Boone because I realize I've been blathering away like a fool and he's been silent as a gravestone.

"What is it?" I ask.

"Never took you for a romantic."

Dammit, why is my face always so hot when I'm around this man? "Not romantic. Just...hopeful."

He shrugs and mutters something that sounds a lot like "romantic" into Pegasus's coat.

The sun has gone all the way down. I nibble on some dried meat and hardtack. Boone removes a cloth-wrapped bundle from one of his saddlebags and pulls it open to reveal a generous loaf of fresh bread and a little jar of berry preserves.

"Where'd you get that?" I ask.

"Mrs. Hardin," he says without any trace of joking.

"She said they didn't have extra to sell," I say, frowning at him. I'd tried to buy some from her after retrieving Kitty and Pegasus.

"Probably because she gave it all to me." He tears off a hunk of bread and uses a long hunting knife, totally inappropriate to the task at hand, to slather some of the preserves onto the bread. "Like I said, it don't cost nothing to be friendly."

I fold my arms across my chest and hope the hardtack softens in my mouth at some point so I can pretend it's something tastier.

"Here." Boone thrusts the preserves-laden chunk of bread at me.

"No, thanks," I say, even though the sweet scent of the preserves lifts to my nose.

"Don't be a mule. Take the damn bread, Boswell. I can hold my arm out like this all night."

Glaring at him, I say, "Thank you," and accept the bread. When I take a bite, it tastes friendly. I'm not sure I like it.

"I assume you have an opinion on who should take first watch," he says around his own mouthful of bread.

I do, but it burrows under my skin like a bedbug that he said so. I say, "It doesn't matter one way or the other."

"Fine," he says slowly, as if he's trying to figure me out. "I'll take first watch, then."

"Fine. Thank you for sharing your bread and preserves."

As soon as I've wolfed down my meal, I grab my bedroll from the saddlebag and lay it out over the grass, doing a quick check for snakes.

It don't take long of me looking at the constellation of the wise woman in her feathered skirt before my mind starts working to remember things. Plenty of memories to be had in the darkness. I wish we could have a little fire, chase off the chill of the night.

Pa used to tell me what life was like before the Rift. Travelers and cowherds would build fires at night, cook over them just like you would in your own kitchen. They could warm their weary bones in the fire's heat, drink a little whiskey if they'd brought it, and tell tales for entertainment.

When the Rift opened, camp fires became a beacon to the preternatural outlaws, and the practice of them stopped entirely. I can only imagine what it was like before, to share stories and warm my belly with whiskey and the heat of a fire.

I miss a life I never had.

———

A HAND on my shoulder wakes me. My knife is in my palm and at the man's throat before my brain catches up and I sit back.

The man in question, Boone, just raises his dark eyebrows and holds a finger up to his lips to signal quiet.

He must hear something. I strain my ears trying to listen, but all I can make out are the chilling howls of coyotes that have to be at least twenty miles away. I send a confused look to Boone.

What seems like ages later, I hear it—a shushing in the grass.

Faster than I can track, Boone's up in the air, racing away. There's a thud, followed by a holler. I hustle through the darkness, able to make out the struggling forms wrestling on the ground. It's impossible to tell which is Boone. Then a plaintive voice says, "It's me, get *off.*"

Boone's off the person lickety-split. He comes over to stand next to me and faces his opponent. "Carson?"

Carson's leaning over, hands on his knees, breathing hard. "Rift take you," he pants. "You didn't have to knock me off my damned horse."

"You knocked him off a horse?" I ask Boone, before looking around. The horse in question has gone to stand next to Pegasus and Kitty, who eye him like they aren't sure he should be allowed to join them.

"He did, and then he nearly strangled me," Carson says. "Why Gracie would be working with someone like you—"

"Shut your yap," Boone says, "or I'll finish what I started with the strangling."

"Boys." Why do I suddenly feel like I'm a parent with two squabbling children? "Enough. Carson, why're you here?"

"I'm a part of your posse," he says. "Whether or not I'm welcome, I made an agreement and I aim to keep it."

"The agreement was null and void soon as you high-tailed it off into town," Boone growls.

"I have a charm here with your name on it, Levi Boone," Carson says, reaching for his holster.

Before Boone can retort, I hold up a hand. Carson's presence seems an annoyance to Boone. And maybe I ain't a good person, but Boone's annoyance is enough to make me want to keep Carson around.

"You threatened to hex Boone," I say to Carson. "I didn't know you sling charms, too."

"I do now," Carson says, shooting a dirty look at Boone. "Bought myself a fair few before I left Penance."

"Carson can stay," I say quietly. "Both of you can rest. I'll take the next watch."

They grumble and throw angry looks at each other, but after Carson tends his horse, he unrolls a mat to sleep on and the two of them settle down about as far from each other—and me—as is safe.

I get comfortable—but not too comfortable—on my bedroll, facing the direction of the rocky foothills, for the most part. Over the course of the next couple of hours, I switch positions and face the flowing plains. Then I switch again, looking out at the brush-filled desert.

Today has been frustrating on more than one count. There's the fact that I'm working with two other fellas, and I don't like company for the most part. Then there's the fact that even with three of us, we could search those craggy hills every day until the Rift closes up and still not find that nest of vampires.

We need a plan—a better plan than just blindly walking around like lost sheep waiting for the wolves to attack.

While the men rest, my mind works just as hard as my eyes, searching for answers while I scan the dark horizon.

NINE

SUNRISE OVER A PRAIRIE has got to be one of the prettiest sights in the world. No Rift can take that away, the orange light glowing over the grass, then reflecting back from the mountains behind us.

I wake and see Boone already up, as he took the last watch. His gaze is rapt on the burnished orange and pink sky. My voice doesn't want to work, so I take care of packing my belongings. Carson's still asleep, flat on his back, hat resting on top of his face.

Boone whistles, loud and sudden, startling a covey of quail. They erupt from the grass with a storm of wings.

Carson jerks to a sitting position, hat falling to the side and hand going for his pistol.

"Sleep well, pup?" Boone says to Carson.

Carson's eyes get wide, then he narrows them at Boone. "Watch your mouth."

I'd appreciate the pretty sunrise a lot more if it were just me and Kitty looking at it, but I have a posse, apparently, so I draw what serenity I can from the picturesque landscape, then kick one of Carson's empty boots as I stride to the horses with my bedroll and saddlebags.

"Everyone up, let's go," I say.

Carson puts on his boots and eases up to standing. He folds his bedroll and turns around to see me watching him at it. He winks. I shake my head. The man can be handsome as Zeus but that don't mean I have a use for him. Not out here. Not when there's work to be done.

We mount our horses and head in the direction of the hills. But when I veer northwest toward Penance, Boone and Carson slow.

"Where are you going?" Carson asks.

"Had an idea last night."

Boone pulls Pegasus up so that he's just a frog's hair ahead of me. "We formed a posse, all three of us. You should tell us what the plan is."

Kitty dances beneath me, sensing the tension in the air. It feels like a storm could be coming, but I know it ain't a storm. It's just the tension of Boone's restrained anger.

I'm not intimidated, but he has a fair point. I'd just rather do than talk, that's all.

"There's a grave site over this way," I say. "Townspeople that the nest killed."

"All right," Carson says slowly, while Boone waits without talking.

"Double crosses on each grave," I continue.

"Because the town was worried they'd rise," Carson says. "Common enough practice after someone's been killed by a vampire, if they don't plan on removing the head."

I nod and thread Kitty's reins between my fingers, one-two-three loops, before unwinding them again. "I'm willing to gamble they didn't burn their loved ones or take off their heads."

"No," Boone says.

"Exactly," I continue, glad to have his support while Carson gives me a clueless prairie dog stare. Now I'm understanding why Boone started calling him *pup*. "So we take a secondary cross from the ground and let one of 'em rise—"

"I mean no, we ain't doing it," Boone says.

Carson's prairie dog eyes get even bigger as he continues to look at me. "You can't be saying—"

"That is exactly what I'm saying," I say, forming a fist with the reins wrapped around my fingers again. There's a bite of pain from the dig of the leather, but it grounds me to the moment so I can think better. "I'm saying we set one free. It'll go right to its sire—that's what they always do."

"But what if it doesn't?" Carson asks. "What if it goes to Penance, instead?"

"It won't do that," I say. "It won't go to the town— they hate going to their old homes."

"Doesn't matter where it goes," Boone says. "However you do this, it's disrespecting the dead."

"Probably a mite better than waiting twenty or so years for someone to forget to replace rotting crosses, and they all rise to terrorize the countryside in search of their sires."

Boone's shaking his head, but Carson says, "Yeah. Let's do it."

Boone is outvoted. Not that this here posse is a democracy. His lips form a thin line across that strong face, but he nudges Pegasus to go along. This time, Carson and I lead the way.

Carson might seem inexperienced, but he rides with confidence, like he's one with his horse. And he might've balked at some of the blood that night in Penance, but he still handled himself, and he staked that vampire.

I still can't believe I froze up. Memories are powerful things, and mine got the best of me, I guess.

Well, not tonight.

It takes us a short while to find the grave site. Seventeen graves, thirty-four crosses. Boone takes off his hat, respectful-like. I do the same, then hiss at Carson until he picks up on our moment of quiet contemplation. I don't know what Boone's thinking about, or Carson, but I think about how one of these soulless haunts is going to take us to our pay day, and I can't wait to get started.

I do wait, though, out of some respect for Boone. He ain't comfortable with this, and even though we're going to do it anyway, it don't hurt to make him a teensy bit less reluctant.

There's a house in the distance I didn't notice last time I was traveling through. Smoke leaves the chimney in cheerful little puffs. I wonder if the family is scared, living this far from town, this close to the Rift.

Eventually, Boone jams his hat back on and says, "Well, I know you're eager to pick one, so just do it."

I put my hat back on and dismount, then walk slowly over to the graves. From the looks of them up close, it seems the townspeople hastily carved names and sometimes dates into each cross that goes at the head. I try not to focus on the names and resolve to just grab one of the chest crosses. When I reach for one, though, I catch a glimpse of the carving on the head cross. There's a name, but there's numbers, too. Years. I do the math.

This was a kid. I let go of the chest cross like it bit me.

"What is it?" Carson asks.

"Nothin'. That just ain't a good one." I grab another cross. No indication on the head that this was a child, so I yank the second cross from the earth.

To the town's credit, the chest cross goes down a good three feet into the soil.

I consider taking out another couple of chest crosses, but I know Boone would object. We can always come back if this person doesn't rise as a vampire, but I am extremely confident they will. *Beatrice*, the head cross reads, and the emblazoned name is a reminder that she was a human, at one point.

I shove that sentiment aside, out of my mind. Doesn't do to dwell on it. We're all human at some point and if we're lucky, we die that way. Beatrice wasn't lucky.

We ride into the rocky foothills and look around while we wait for the day to pass. We don't find anything except a rattler and the tracks of what could almost be a coyote print, but Boone says is actually a wolf.

"Wolves don't come around these parts," I say.

"Shapeshifter," he says.

My understanding was that when the shapeshifters came from the Rift, they spread far and wide. Frowning, I say, "I didn't think they came around these parts, either."

"They're closer than you think." Boone's voice holds a note of warning in it.

"What's this?" Carson asks, gesturing me over to his side.

I scramble over a rock face, hoping he's finally found us a track or a clue. In my haste, I lose my footing. Dammit, I'm sliding. There's a bare branch close by, a dead bush. I flail for it, make contact, close my fist around dry bark. It doesn't hold my weight, though. I keep sliding. The fall won't kill me, but it won't feel great, either. Wincing, I brace for the landing.

But then Carson's hand is gripping my other wrist, solid and sure, and my descent halts.

"I got you," he says, slowly pulling me up.

I push against the rock with my heels, helping ease my weight in his grasp, but he's barely panting as he hauls me toward him.

Carson's stronger than he looks. Boone might need to rethink that "pup" nickname.

When I'm up the rock face, I sag against the next boulder, gulping breaths. I wasn't gonna die, I remind myself. It was just gonna hurt. That's all. A mending stone would've fixed me up in no time. But my fool heart doesn't seem to realize that, and it's still pounding like I had a foot in the grave.

"What'd you find, pup?" Boone asks.

"Thought there was a footprint or something over here," Carson says. "But it's gone now. Must've been a trick of the light."

"Sure," Boone says.

"Speaking of the light," I say, noting the way the hillside has fallen into shadow, "we should get back to the grave site. Sun's going down."

We make our way down the hill to where the horses are tied, and ride back to the rows of crosses.

"We need to get downwind of the graves," Boone said, "so as the vampire doesn't smell us."

"They can *smell* us?" I ask. "I never heard such a thing."

"Your hand is bleeding. Vampires can smell blood."

I hadn't even noticed, but sure enough, there's a small cut and some blood on my right hand. I must've sliced it on the rock when I slid down, or maybe on the branch I tried to grab.

We figure out the direction of the breeze and put ourselves in a better position. I nibble some dried berries and we wait for night to fall. My eyes don't leave the grave in the group that has a single cross on it. The second cross, I tossed off to the side, carelessly, and I make a mental note to put it back in the ground next time I travel this way. The family shouldn't have to worry about what happened to that one.

Carson sidles up next to me, a long blade of grass sticking out of his mouth.

"Why d'you chew on that?" I ask. "It can't taste good."

"I used to smoke," he says. "This gives me something else to do."

"Why'd you stop smoking?"

"The scent bothered my ma, gave her headaches. She's since passed, but I figure, if it bothered her, it might bother others. No sense in picking up the habit again."

"That's mighty thoughtful," I say.

He shrugs. "I know people call me lazy. Maybe they're correct. But I do try to do what's right."

I can't fault him for that. If more people tried, I reckon this territory would be a hell of a lot more pleasant and safe to live in.

When the sun is all the way down, I find that I'm holding my breath.

"See anything yet?" Carson asks.

"Shh," I say.

Boone lifts a single hand and points at the graves.

There it is—a disturbance in the soil, like I imagine the beginnings of the Rift itself. A rippling of the earth before a single hand comes punching up, ready to take the bounty offered by the desert prairie—a bounty of blood.

The hand is splotched with dirt. As I watch in awestruck silence, a second hand joins it, pushing away soil before the rest of the vampire emerges, head first. Its hair used to be light in color. Blond, I think, until the vampire emerges and I realize it's white. Beatrice was once an elderly woman.

Someone's grandma. Not a kid. I exhale.

It doesn't glance in our direction, instead moving toward the foothills. We wait, allowing some distance to form between the vampire and us. I pause before nudging Kitty forward. I almost ask Boone whether he thinks we should start moving, and then I angrily tell myself that I am the one in charge of this posse, and second-guessing my every move isn't the sign of a leader.

I make a soft clicking sound with my tongue to Kitty, and she starts forward at a walk.

Boone and Carson follow suit.

The vampire is fast, moving at a run, its long hair streaming behind it, glowing white in the moonlight as the dirt breaks free. Grasses move in its wake, an upside-down V of dangerous intent.

"Good thinking," Boone says quietly from beside me. "I don't like any part of this, truly, but you're right—she's trying to join her sire."

"How do you know?" Carson asks.

Boone shrugs. "I just do."

I don't question him, because this was my expectation, anyway. The vampire's doing exactly what I'd hoped it would do. Tonight, we'll find the nest. We'll stake the vampires, hopefully find those kids alive and mostly unharmed. I didn't say it to Mrs. Browning, but sometimes the vampires will keep people alive as a source of food, just like a family will keep a cow to milk. So there's a chance more'n one of those kids is alive.

The grasses grow thinner and thinner as we leave the river's reach, until we're traveling over dirt, winding through brush. We keep the horses from running because we don't want to overtake the vampire or alert it to our presence. Instead of heading up the first hill, where we did most of our searching yesterday and today, the vampire skirts around it.

"Yah," I say to Kitty, squeezing her sides. She breaks into a lope.

We ride for a couple hours. I squint in the dark shadows along the lower edge of a foothill. We can't lose the vampire, otherwise we've just welcomed another bloodsucker into the world for no reason at all. We navigate through a thick copse of trees. The vampire's long hair helps us along, like a flag beckoning us onward. We step over logs, a low creek, and press through brush. I jump off of Kitty and wrap her reins around a tree branch. She'll be able to free herself if I don't make it out of here, but she'll also know to stay a spell and wait for me.

Boone and Carson secure their horses, as well. I spy the vampire walking through the piles of rocks, picking its way along with more speed than I'm capable of on similar terrain. We're going to have to move fast.

Boone's right behind me, Carson a few steps back. We move as quickly as possible, and I lose all sense of time.

The vampire is focused on its own progress and still hasn't seen us. I scramble over one rock, then another. Any rattlers around here will be sleepier than at midday, but the rocks still hold some of the sun's heat, and they'll be warm enough to bite if disturbed. I place my hands and feet as carefully as possible.

It must be hours of scrambling and sometime after midnight when the vampire changes direction, moving up the hill instead of along the bottom. The smaller, person-sized rocks have given way for larger boulders, reducing our visibility.

"Hurry up," I whisper to the other two, and my scrambling becomes in earnest, one hand, one foot, quickly overtaking each other as I make my way over the boulders. Sometimes I'm outright climbing, and I'm no longer careful about where my hands and feet go, just praying all the snakes are hiding somewhere else, on some other warm rock.

My muscles are straining, my body fatigued. I wonder if the vampire will reach its sire before dawn.

I'm afraid to take my gaze off the vampire, but I risk a look back to see how Boone and Carson are faring. They aren't far behind. Satisfied, I return to my own progress. I pass a cavern that might make a hiding spot for a nest of vampires, but that ain't where this vampire is going, so I hurry past it.

Boone's not as quiet as me, and I hear a scuffling of boot against rock. When I turn around to tell him to keep it down, I see that he's turning around, too. The scuffling sound wasn't Boone—it was Carson.

Someone's holding him, arm around his neck, and dragging him. The scuff was his leg kicking out as he tried to get our attention.

He's got our attention now, as does the fiend choking him.

TEN

THE VAMPIRE STANDING behind Carson grins, revealing sharp fangs. Its hold on Carson seems effortless, as if it could stand in this position all night without tiring. Carson's blue eyes are wide, his hands scrambling at the arm that holds him. He scrapes the bloodsucker's forearm with his fingernails, but the vampire doesn't seem to feel the gouges or care.

The vampire was on the wanted poster, the fresh-faced adolescent, one of those without a name. It had looked so harmless with its youthful features. That notion of harmlessness disappears quickly as the vampire lowers its mouth to Carson's neck. "I have to save you for the master. But first, a taste, I think..."

Kicking his legs, Carson tries to gain some purchase. If he could just reach something, he could slam the vampire back into the boulder behind him. But the vampire, while smaller than him, has the kind of grip no man can escape.

Boone pulls a stake from his thigh sheath and I do the

same. The stakes are charmed for accuracy and speed, but when there are two possible targets, the stakes don't always make the right call. I take aim with mine, and the point of the stake wavers between the vampire and Carson. Yeah, that ain't gonna work. Best to do the job by gun.

The vampire's smart, holds Carson in front of it. My pistol is steady in my hand. The gun, too, is charmed with accuracy, but not to the point it'll interfere with my selected target. A stake would've been better, because the charm in here'll only stun a being, not kill it.

I sense Boone doing the same with his own pistol. He moves to the side at the same time, trying for a better angle.

It's hard to see color in the night, even with my sight charm, but Carson's face is reddening. He's losing oxygen fast. The vampire likely won't kill him, but I'd rather Carson not pass out—it's best for us all if he's still able to fight, even in this position.

The trigger's cool against my index finger. I match up the vampire's shoulder with the sights and everything else comes second-nature. I squeeze the trigger. The charm shoots out in a line of green light. It momentarily ruins my night vision, but Boone's already moving while I blink away the afterglow. A faint tinge of magic fills the air— smoky and otherworldly. Already I can feel the beginnings of a headache.

When I can see again, both Boone and Carson are standing over the stunned vampire, and Boone's saying, "Tell us where the nest is hiding."

The vampire blinks, opens its mouth to reveal its fangs, and hisses. "Never."

"We could make your final death fast or slow," Carson says, pulling a knife from a sheath on his belt.

"Better make it fast," the vampire says with a dry chuckle. Its attention flicks to the sky above us.

A boulder overhangs from above, and standing on it are the new vampire, Beatrice, and a second one that I assume is the sire, flanked by four others.

I'd suspected there were more than four bloodsuckers in the nest, and this confirms it.

They have the high ground, the numbers, all of the advantage now. What we had going for us was the element of surprise, and now we've lost it.

We need to run.

The vampire on the ground uses our distraction to sweep my legs out from under me. The boulders surrounding me seem to tilt as I fall, but I catch myself on one of them. The vampire's moving fast, trying to get behind me like it did Carson, but I punch out with my left arm, straightening it back from the elbow, and I jab my stake into the vampire's heart.

Boone uses a knife that must be sharper than anything to slice through the vampire's neck. The head topples off. Now it's deader than dead. Then Boone's dragging me up to standing and he, Carson, and I are running as best we can over the rocks and boulders. I curse under my breath with every footstep.

We failed. It should not have come to this, and I want to wallow in that regret like a pig cooling itself in mud, but the regret won't help us get out of this situation.

Running feels wrong. Running gives them another night to terrorize the prairie and its towns.

But running also gives us another day to survive and come up with a new plan.

I don't have to like it, but I have to recognize it's the right call.

A wind picks up, whipping my braid around my back. Trees around us creak in the gale. Every movement causes me to reach for my gun, thinking that the vampires have caught up to us.

Thankfully, that ain't the case, and the vampires trail behind as they pursue us down the hill. I turn to look once, and they're a few yards away. Then I look again and they're farther back, pausing on one of the larger boulders. They stop there, so I stop, too.

"What are they doing?" I murmur to myself. My voice is yanked away by the wind. I hate that the nest is bigger than the wanted poster proclaimed. Plus, we gave them a new one tonight. Took one, too, so I s'pose that makes us even.

Boone says, "They're doing the same as we are. Coming up with a new strategy. And the sun'll be rising soon, so they can't chase us too far out into the open."

Carson swears. "I didn't know the bloodsuckers had the brains for strategies."

"What you don't know could fill an ocean," Boone says, his voice sharp.

"Enough, you two," I say. "Let's get out of here."

I turn to go. Boone catches up and matches me step for step, his broad shoulders throwing shadow in the moonlight.

"Wait," Boone says, holding up a hand.

The only thing I can hear is my breathing and the pounding of my heart.

"What is it?" Carson asks in a soft voice.

I'm scared, which makes me impatient. I want to turn around and attack those vampires chasing us, but I know we're far outnumbered and at an extreme disadvantage. But Boone's still looking around, hand held up in warning. He turns around until he faces a rock some yards behind us.

I turn and follow his gaze. There's a vampire standing on the rock. It steps forward and raises its hand in the mockery of a greeting.

"I have a message for you, bounty hunter," it says. The form wears no hat, yet its face is in shadow.

"Who are you?" I ask.

"Don't you know all about me? Am I not on your wanted poster?" It raises its head, and the barest wisps of moonlight shine upon it. Its fangs are the first things I notice. Sharp, gleaming.

I recognize the vampire now. John Marlowe. The sketch on the poster was an accurate likeness, from its high forehead to its pointy beard. Most especially, the anger in its dark eyes.

"You might want to take your nest and get out of this territory," I tell the vampire, reaching for my pistol with one hand and a stake with the other. "You ain't welcome here."

I blink, and it's gone. The rock is bare.

"Where'd he go?" Carson asks.

"I'm everywhere," the voice says.

Carson and I jump, startled, but Boone keeps scanning the trees around us. The vampire can't be far.

"You can leave here, and live," the voice says. "Leave this little patch of woods, leave these dry hills, leave the city of silver. Because the vampires are taking Penance and all the humans who live there. They shall be our cattle, and Penance shall be a vampire town."

"That'll never happen," Carson says, although his face is pale in the blue-gray light of the growing dawn.

The vampire goes on, "We'll no longer be considered outlaws. The town will be ours."

Shadows flit this way and that in the trees, growing closer to where we stand.

The vampire and its allies are surrounding us.

I nudge Carson and Boone, and we start walking, fast as possible, putting as much distance between us and the shadows as we can. We find the horses, leap onto their backs, and tear out of the woods.

Once we get to the desert plains and the brush and brambles, it's easier to see. Shadows can't loom like they did beneath the tree branches.

"Are they following?" I shout to Boone, who's pulling up the rear.

He turns, looks, then faces me again. "No."

"You sure?"

"I'm sure. Dawn's coming. We're safe." Then Boone turns and stares hard at Carson. "Why'd you get so close to that cavern entrance, anyway?"

"Gracie blazed right past it," Carson says. "I didn't give it a second thought."

Both men look at me.

"It didn't seem important to me at the time. I was intent on following our new vampire." I don't know why I feel the need to explain myself to them. The growing wind steals the heat from my person and I shiver. This is my mission. And yet, my inattention on the surroundings signaled to Carson that he didn't need to worry about a potential danger. Clenching my fists, I say, "Let's get out of here."

My mind is churning, one thought circling back to another, as I try to come up with a plan for tomorrow night.

Nothing I hate more than retreating, tail between my legs like a sorry puppy.

Instead of returning to the prairie where we rested last night, I continue through the forest of stunted junipers, gripping the saddle horn like it'll keep me present in the moment. Thunder rumbles in the distance, matching my mood. Last thing I need is an early summer storm, drenching us and destroying all the vampire tracks.

We dismount, and Carson comes up on the side of me. "It ain't your fault, Gracie. I know to look at things with my own two eyes."

"This is why I don't want a posse," I say. One of many reasons. "I don't want to be responsible for people getting hurt."

"We're responsible for ourselves," Boone says from behind me.

There's a creek ahead, which explains the extra greenery.

I spin around. "Forget running. We need to get back

up there, track those vampires before they can move again."

"What?" Carson says. "It's starting to rain, Gracie."

"I'm aware."

"It's going to storm." He holds out a hand as raindrops begin falling—sideways, bent that way by the wind.

"We need to wait," Boone says. "They won't get far if they try to move their camp. Even under clouds, they're still affected by sunlight. They won't risk it."

I kick the base of a juniper and fold my arms over my chest, partly to show my displeasure, partly to hold in some of my body heat. Boone's right. Damn him, he's right. Carson, too.

"Fine. We'll camp here," I say. Now that dawn's upon us, we'll be safe while we figure out our next move. We're not far from the grave site, either. I can go back, pull another cross from the ground, start again.

This time, without the advantage of surprise.

Boone and Carson are quiet as we take care of the horses and set up our bedrolls. Rain spatters us, leaving wet drop patterns on our hats and clothes. Everyone's mood sours. Ain't no fun sleeping out in the open in general, but it's downright miserable when everything's wet.

We've been awake for a full day and a full night, and if Boone and Carson are anything like me, they're feeling the fatigue.

Raindrops come down faster, slamming against my hat with harsh thwacking sounds. Yanking my hat down farther, I try to keep them off my neck as much as possible.

"I'll take first watch," I say, because ain't no way my mind is going to quiet enough for sleep any time soon.

Carson settles onto his sleeping roll. As if the rain don't mean nothing to him, he places his hat over his face and is snoring within seconds. Boone doesn't lay himself down; instead he sits up, legs out in front of him, boots still on. His light brown eyes assess me and I look away, toward the flowing waters of the creek where the rain smacks into it, leaving the flashes of little divots in the dawn light.

"You're not gonna like my idea for tomorrow," I say to Boone as I spread out my own bedroll and sit on it.

"Reckon I won't, if you already know it," he says.

Forcing my gaze back to his, I say, "I want to do the same thing again. Free a vampire. We follow, we don't engage, we just see where it's going, quiet-like."

He's already shaking his head, and I feel my anger flare. I don't want to be loud and wake up Carson, and shouting never worked for me, anyway. My preference is to go low, quiet.

"Shake your head all you want, Levi Boone, but this is the best plan there is. I've thought through all the rest, and none of 'em are any better."

"Boswell."

Ignoring him, I go on, "Unless you brought some other charms to sling that can help us find a nest of vampires in caverns we can't locate?"

No such tracking charms exist that I'm aware. I've never needed one before, though, so I've never thought to ask.

We could start a hill on fire if this rain lets up, try to

flush them out. Trap 'em in a canyon, maybe, with flames. But if they have any of those Browning siblings in their clutches, it would put the humans in danger, too.

"Following a new vampire to its sire is the best option," I say to myself. "Just because it didn't work before doesn't mean it won't work this time."

My duster is already soaked through, the chill of the rain seeping through my shirt. I try to ignore the cold, focus on my argument.

"Boswell."

I flinch—not because Boone's tone is harsh, but because it's somber. "What?"

"Boswell, those are peoples' family, in the ground."

"Yes, I know. It happens sometimes. Family gets killed. It's awful, but we have to move on."

Those are the thoughts I had, the talking-to I gave myself, after Pa died. People die, every day. Whether it's from an illness, or an accident, or an attack. And the survivors get through it. Sometimes, with help. Or sometimes, their neighbors don't have the time or inclination to care. Sometimes, their neighbors no longer trust them. Sometimes, they grieve alone.

Instead of saying these things, I say, "If we didn't die, we wouldn't be human."

"We also need to act with compassion," he says in a soft voice, his eyes never leaving mine. "Ain't nothing more human than that."

Tears clog my throat, like I'm parched all of a sudden. I'm tempted to open my mouth and tilt my face up to gulp the water raining from the heavens. Instead, I stare hard at the banks of the creek, the tangle of juniper brush that surrounds it.

"Compassion gets people killed," I say. "It's dangerous."

I think the groaning trees might cover up my words, but Boone raises a single eyebrow.

"Like friendliness?" he asks. It's a reminder of our conversation that first morning, and another moment where I'd come around to at least begrudgingly accept his perspective.

Damn him. I don't want friendliness, I don't want compassion. I want to do a good job, capably.

"You take first watch," I say in a rush as I scramble to my feet. "I need a moment."

The words *I need a moment* generally convey a body's need to relieve themselves somewhere privately, so I'm surprised when Boone kicks Carson awake with a gruff, "Your watch, pup," and follows me over to the creek.

Carson groans and rolls over, not getting up, but I can see his eyes are open. Then I turn away to face the creek so I don't have to look at him or Boone.

Boone stands next to me while I stare at the darkly rushing water. I swallow past the thickness in my throat, then swallow again. I can't seem to get rid of the tightness. I'm not often grateful to the wind for anything, but I'm grateful right now that it's hiding the sound of my ragged breaths.

Boone makes a soft noise, and I think it's meant to be comforting, but if I could speak, I'd tell him to close his mouth and close it good. I don't want comfort, and I don't want friendliness.

I haven't cried in front of anyone since my pa died, and I don't aim to start now.

"Boswell," Boone says.

That's what he's been saying—my name. The way he says it sounds all soft, like mullein leaves. He's never called me Gracie, always Boswell, but somehow the way his mouth forms the syllables makes my last name sound more gentle than my first.

I look over at him—not up to his face, because I don't want to see the kindness in his eyes. I can hear it well enough in his voice, and it hurts just as much as meanness. Instead I focus on the bend in his knee, the way the brown fabric ripples there just behind it, the way raindrops make patterns of darkness on the material.

"Do you want to talk, Boswell?" he asks.

I shake my head.

He reaches for me slowly—slowly enough I could get away if I wanted. And getting away sounds nice, because the big feelings growing right now are a little more than I can bear to think about. His arms are warm about my shoulders. He takes in a long breath, holds it, then lets it out. Then he does it again.

I start to feel calmer. I feel less like a monster and more like a woman who has a job to do.

"We can try it your way, if you have a better idea," I say. "But I'm not entirely ruling out a return to the graves. We did see the vampires today. That's a success. The number of them—could you count 'em, Boone?"

"At least eight," he says. "Maybe more."

"That's what I saw." I sigh. The vampire's threats echo in my head. They want to take Penance as their own. We can't let that happen. "As soon as this storm's over, we go back up that hill."

"They can't have gotten far. And Boswell, you're doing a good job. I hope you don't mind me saying so. I'm glad you're in charge of this posse."

I'm capable of this, and Boone's right—I'm capable of doing it without desecrating any more graves.

Just because the folks of Penance should've dealt with their dead differently doesn't mean I have a right to use the bodies, vampires or not.

Stepping out of Boone's embrace, I open my mouth to say thank you, maybe, or tell him that he's right about this and I appreciate his vote of confidence. Honestly, I ain't sure what I aim to say, because before I can get out a sound, something grabs my ankle.

ELEVEN

I GIVE a shout of surprise and kick backward, trying to dislodge the thing that holds me, but its grip is strong. I can feel the individual fingers through the thick leather of my boot.

Boone's eyes grow big and he grabs my elbows.

It's got to be a fae, but I'm too afraid to look.

"Don't let go of me," Boone says, "no matter what."

I don't have time to ask him what he means, because a second hand grips my other ankle and I'm pulled taut between Boone and the fae.

Doesn't take me long to realize why this is happening. I didn't throw any hardtack into the water. We crossed this creek when we came into the woods, and I wasn't paying attention to anything except that vampire's words and my own failures.

"Gracie!" Carson runs over, all shadow and speed in the brightening dawn. His hat is gone, left behind on his bedroll, and he's not even wearing his boots—a risky move in these parts.

When a third hand grabs me by the knee, I know I'm a goner. The fae has me in its grip, and ain't no way three humans can fight it.

I'm suspended over the bank of the creek, afraid to look down at what holds my feet. But knowing it is the only chance I have of fighting it. Sucking in a breath, I look down. The hands that hold my legs are made of webbed fingers, and they look red. These are blood stains that no amount of water will ever wash away. As I watch, a fourth arm emerges from the rushing creek and coils itself around my waist.

Carson's holding one of my arms, Boone the other. My back cracks, and my shoulders are straining. If I stretch too much more, my shoulder bones are going to pop out of place.

"Knife," Boone gasps. "I can hold her. Get my knife and cut off the arm around her waist."

Carson nods and I lift my head so I can see him free the knife from Boone's belt. He slashes out, cutting into the slick, red arm that holds me about the waist. The fae recoils, pulling me closer to the water. I keep my head down, eyes on the toes of Boone's boots and Carson's bare feet. It's been a long time since I saw another soul's bare feet, and for some crazy-ass reason, my mind focuses on the fact that Carson's feet are rather nice. The toes are well-proportioned, and they look strong. If it's possible for a cowherd to have a noble set of feet, then Carson does.

Both sets of feet slide forward as the fae drags me to the water.

These men are going to get sucked in after me if they keep trying to save me.

Carson gets the fae's arm loose from around my waist, but a fifth arm shoots out of the water and nearly misses him. It grips my shoulder instead. Carson gets to work slicing at it, sometimes getting my shoulder in the process, but I ain't complaining.

"You two need to let me go and get out of here," I say, gritting my teeth against the pain of being stretched. "Toss some hardtack into the creek before you cross it on your way out."

"We ain't letting you go," Carson says furiously, slashing at the hand holding my shoulder.

"Neither is this fae," I say. "Either I get—pulled in half—or we all go into that water."

"No." Boone's voice is low, determined. He ain't barely breaking a sweat, he's a picture of control as he holds me fast with one hand and takes a pistol from a second holster and comes around the side of me.

I've no idea how he can hold me as tight now as he was before with just one hand and this new, awkward angle, but I ain't going to question it. I look down toward my feet to see him aiming at one of the hands on my ankle.

He fires the pistol. It isn't a charm—it's a metal bullet.

A shrieking sound of pain comes from the stream.

"You have a gun?" I ask. "A real gun?"

Everything hurts. A dip in the water don't sound too bad anymore. I could do with a wash, anyway. The thought makes me giggle. "I needed a bath," I say, laughing at the hilarity of it.

"Its magic is getting into her head," Carson says.

"Yeah, I know," Boone says, taking aim and firing again.

With a snap, my right leg is free. Water sloshes angrily behind me.

The easing of the pressure in my leg and hips brings a little sense back into me. I don't want to die. I don't want to go in that water to taste the fae's kiss.

Another arm shoots out of the water near my feet.

"You got her?" Carson shouts.

"Yes," Boone answers.

Carson lets go of me, grabs his pistol, and takes aim. A spell flashes out of the barrel and hits the new arm.

The thing about the fae is they aren't usually much bothered by witch magic. But after having its arms hacked off and shot with both bullets and a charm, this fae seems to have had enough. It releases my other foot.

I fall forward as Boone falls back, then I'm on top of him. We're both panting. My whole body feels stretched and achy, like my muscles have forgotten where they belong on my frame. Still, the feelings of terror and struggle are rocking through me, and I shudder.

I almost died in a watery grave, brought down by the same kind of fae that killed my dog when I was a girl.

All because I forgot to share some of my hardtack with it.

My body continues to shake, and I'm mad enough to spit. Boone brings an arm around my back, like it's an embrace. The shaking subsides and I look down at him, his face just inches from mine. His gaze flicks to my mouth and my heart stutters in my chest.

I've kissed a man once, and it started like this. Bodies pressed close, the glance at the mouth. Boone's lips look soft. A kiss wouldn't be unwelcome, even if it was coming from Levi Boone. Maybe it would be even more welcome from Levi Boone.

Carson clears his throat, and I scramble off of Boone, my face hot. Making my way to my bedroll, I sit down with an exhausted thump. I find a piece of hardtack in my saddlebag and fling it in the direction of the creek. I'll make a more proper gesture tomorrow, when my temper's had time to cool off some.

Boone and Carson are quiet, and I'm grateful. Rain patters gently against the grass, and the wind has died somewhat.

Then Carson says, "So...whose watch is it?"

———

I WAKE to an orangish-yellow sunlight streaming through the juniper branches nearest me. Can't have been more than an hour or two of sleep this morning. Turning on my side makes me feel like I've been dragged behind a horse. I let forth a string of curses.

"You kiss your ma with that mouth?" Carson asks.

"Never kissed my ma," I say, standing up with difficulty.

"That explains it," he says.

All traces of the storm are gone, other than a dampness in the grass that wasn't there before.

Boone's sitting off to the side, hat pulled low on his

forehead while he reads a thick book in his hands. He notices me looking and says, "It's a Bible."

"Really," I say.

"Really."

"You some kind of preacher or something?" I ask.

Carson guffaws.

"It's a real question," I say, turning to Carson. "I ain't making fun of him. Why are you?"

Boone slams the book shut. "We should get going."

I don't have to think hard to guess what he wants to do. But I'm the one in charge, and it bruises my dignity he'd try to be the leader.

"We ain't far from the hill where we found 'em last night." I give my back an experimental stretch and mutter an oath. It feels like someone ripped out all my muscles and bones, then jammed them backwards into my body again. "It's the obvious place to start."

"So we're not going to follow another one from those new graves?" Carson asks.

"No." I pull my pistol from its holster and reload the cylinder with activated stunner charms. I wish I'd had time to clean it before leaving for this hunt, but maybe there'll be time tonight. It'll function fine without the cleaning, but messing with all the parts soothes me.

It reminds me of Boone shooting off a bullet—a real bullet—last night.

"You have two pistols," I say to him.

He nods.

"I do, too," Carson says.

"I don't like bullets," I say.

"You don't have to use them." Boone's voice is matter-of-fact.

Irritated, I fiddle with my pistol, checking the cylinder. All the rounds are full, charms ready to go before I risk a glance at the men. Carson's giving me a strange look, and Boone ain't looking at anything much.

We ready our horses. As I buckle in my saddlebags, I pull a packet of hardtack from one of them. I pop a piece in my mouth and take the other over to the creek.

"Don't get too close," Carson says.

"I know," I say, frowning. Feeling spooked, I toss the extra piece of hardtack into the water.

Did I merely imagine it, or did a crimson hand emerge from beside one of the rocks to snatch up the floating beige square? I hope the fae and me are even now, but it's hard to imagine I'm worth the same to it as a piece of hardtack.

"Let's ride," I say, marching back to Kitty and the others.

We travel some ways. It's long enough for my aches and pains to scream at me, but not long enough for me to ask the others to stop on my account. My pride is worth something. I find some dried berries in another packet in my saddlebag and I chew them slowly, relishing their sweetness. Carson opens his mouth and waggles his eyebrows at me, so I throw one in his direction. He catches it in his mouth and smiles.

As we pass through the stunted trees, sunlight streams through branches, dappling our skin. It bends around Boone in that queer way it does sometimes, and I think again of when I fell on top of him after the fae attack.

I would've kissed him if Carson hadn't reminded me that Boone and I weren't alone. I don't know whether to thank Carson or shoot him.

TWELVE

BOONE'S in the lead and his back straightens all of a sudden. Immediately, I go on the alert, too, and then I hear it—more horses, the sound of hooves on the ground. I reach for my pistol. Boone does the same in front of me, Carson at my side.

We're close enough to the newcomers now that I can see the colors of their horses' coats as they move through the juniper trees. One horse is white, the other brown, a third one dark brown, almost black. No other horses that I can see.

Three riders. We can deal with that.

"It's the sheriff," Boone says quietly.

"The sheriff?" I ask, then nudge Kitty into a lope.

"Miss Boswell," the sheriff says when I reach her. "I've come to help, and I've brought Wesley, here, as well as Mr. Hardin."

I glance at Mr. Hardin, the barkeep. What good could he possibly be out here? Shaking my head, I say,

"But what about watching over Penance? Seems to me you'd do a bit more good there than out here."

Her gray eyes exhibit sorrow. "I couldn't help the town last night. Vampires even got past the militia. They came so close to dawn I never would've seen it coming."

So close to dawn. That was right around the time the bloodsucker was spouting its threats and chasing us out of the foothills.

There are more than eight vampires in this nest. Hell.

Sheriff goes on, "I put my first deputy in charge and came to you fast as possible. Hardin and I know these hills, we played in them as kids, before the Rift. And Wesley volunteered to assist us in any way he can."

I look at Wesley, who can't be older than nineteen or twenty. The beginnings of a mustache tickle his upper lip, and his chin bears an acne scar or two. The leather of his holster looks stiff, his pistol shiny. He's so full of that aching, youthful confidence that my gold's on him to be the first to die.

Then again, I'm the one who nearly got eaten by a fae this morning.

"What's the goings-on here?" Sheriff asks.

"We found the nest last night," I say, carefully leaving out our method. I don't expect she'd be too pleased with that. "But I regret to tell you that we weren't able to bring any of them down, except one. There are more'n I was led to believe."

I said that last bit without any trace of accusation, but Sheriff bristles in her saddle. "We drew up the ones we saw, for the poster. Ain't no accounting for their ranks growing in the meantime, or them holding vampires back."

Holding up my palm, I say, "Wasn't pointing any fingers, Sheriff. Just noticing this is a bigger bite than I intended to chew off. And no, I ain't asking for more gold, either."

"Ain't you?" Hardin asks.

"She said she ain't," Carson says.

Hardin frowns. Sheriff and Wesley are quiet.

Boone speaks up for the first time. "We're burning daylight."

My impulse is to send Sheriff, Wesley, and Hardin on their way home to Penance. I don't want to be responsible for any more souls on this hunt. But first off, Sheriff has knowledge of these hills, and second, I learned last night that despite the rankling feeling of responsibility for others, I can sometimes use their help, just as they can use mine.

Remains to be seen if they all double-cross me before this is over.

"You're still the leader of this posse," Sheriff says, as if sensing my hesitation.

My leadership ain't what concerns me in the grand scheme. It's their safety, and mine.

"No going into any caves alone like a damned hero," I say.

"Got it," Sheriff says.

"No crossing *any* moving water without throwing in a piece of hardtack," I say.

"Got it," Sheriff says again.

"We take no prisoners," I say. "You see a vampire, you

kill it. No questions, no interrogations. We're taking no chances."

Sheriff nods. "I got that, too. Wesley? Hardin?"

"Got it," Wesley says, touching the unworn leather of his holster.

Hardin nods. "Got it."

I flick Kitty's reins. "Let's ride. We encountered the vampires on that hill, there. Reckon you know where the caverns are on that one?"

"Reckon we do," Hardin says from behind his bushy beard.

Sheriff, Hardin, and Wesley turn their horses around to fall in with us. Carson hesitates.

"Time to go, pup," Boone says to Carson.

Pup. If anyone should have that nickname, it should be young Wesley, whose face is so pale he looks like he came out from behind his ma's skirts just yesterday.

Sheriff comes over to ride alongside me. "You look a little worse for wear," she says.

"Reckon I do. A lesser water fae nearly pulled me into that creek over yonder."

Her silver eyes widen. "I never heard of a body surviving that kind of encounter."

"I got lucky with Boone and Carson here. They held onto me and hacked a few of the creature's arms."

She whistles low.

"Yep," I agree.

"You sure you don't have some kind of charm that helps you cheat death?" she asks, eyeing the bracelets on my wrist.

"Just powerful healing charms, is all," I say.

"You look like you could use some healing now," she says.

"These are for when I'm eyeballing the gates of hell," I say, touching the warm beads. "I'm just uncomfortable now, is all."

She nods. "So that wasn't your first brush with death, I'm guessing. Given your line of work and all."

"No, ma'am. Not my first or second."

"I reckon you've got a lot of stories."

"Reckon you do, too, bein' a sheriff and all."

She nods. "I've brushed up close to death more'n once."

"Fae?" I ask. Other than vampires, they're the most often responsible for preternatural creature attacks—that people survive. If the sheriff had a demon story, we'd be having this conversation in hell.

"A fae courted me for a season."

"Courted you?" I ask. "How in the Rift did it do that?"

She snorts. "He was a perfect gentleman. All kinds of glamour and charms together they can use to disguise a body. Sometimes I wonder if more of them walk among us than we ever know."

My mind travels back to the town of Shepherd, where the fae woman had walked, disguised, right past their marshal.

"Did he have ill intentions?" I ask.

"Turns out, yes, he did, at least at first. My pa angered him somehow—over water rights, now that I think of it—and he popped on some disguise and started comin' around my porch."

"How'd you escape him?" I ask.

"Never took a shining to him," she says simply. "He was handsome as anything, handsomer than Carson, here. But something seemed wrong. Guess it was a gut feeling saved me in the end. He got angry that I didn't like him the same as he said he liked me, and his true form flashed in front of me."

"Did you have to fight him?" I ask.

"No." She taps her lower lip. "Strangest thing. He said he'd come to have feelings, and that he would leave so as to avoid 'complications.' I always wondered what that meant."

Her story's on my mind as she directs us to the closest hill. Sounds to me like that fae developed feelings for her, which is the strangest thing I ever heard. An outlaw falling in love with a human? Preposterous.

Sheriff and Hardin argue over where a specific cavern ought to be, and whether it would be large enough to hold eight or more vampires.

"It was hardly big enough to hold two kids," Hardin says.

"I remember it much bigger than that," Sheriff says, a frown on her face.

Hardin shrugs. "If you say so. I do believe the cave's entrance is on the south side of this here hill, but we can search the other side if you want."

"We'll try this one first, if you're certain." Sheriff has already dismounted. She loops her reins over a juniper bush.

Hardin starts walking up the hillside, barely looking one way or the other. I'd shout for him to stop, but being so loud would wake any outlaw within a fifty-mile radius.

Hurrying to catch up with him, I whisper, "You need to slow down. Rushing up the hill this way is gonna get your blood drained faster than you can say *vampire*."

He worries his lip in his teeth, barely visible through his beard. His hat's pulled so low, I can't see his eyes. I can imagine they're full of disdain as he says, "I don't know why I should take any advice from you, charm-slinger."

Oh, this is delightful. He truly cannot abide magic. I wonder why Sheriff brought him along, if he's going to act like this and generally be a thorn in my backside.

"You don't need to take my advice, or benefit from the magic I use," I say. "But it could save your life. So I hope you remember that."

He resumes his fast-paced hike up the side of the hill, face forward, chin set.

Frowning, I hurry after him. I don't care about saving his skin, but I liked his wife, and he has a son. They'll want him to come home, even if he is stupider than a rock.

"I know that cave is around here somewhere," Hardin mutters from behind his gray-brown beard.

The others follow behind us on what I'm starting to think is a wild, fruitless chase. We scramble after him for a few hours, as he insists over and over that the cave must be close.

Looking at the sky, and where we stand on the hill, I say, "We need to head back down."

Thanks to Hardin, this entire afternoon has been a

waste of time. I can't help but think how much farther along I'd be if I was working alone.

Or maybe I'd just be farther into the bottom of that river, bones picked clean of flesh.

We make our way back down the rocky hillside. It don't take me long to catch up with the others, and I hear Hardin behind. His steps are louder than any of the rest of us. I fall back to step beside him.

"Hey, keep it down," I whisper. "Are you trying to get us found by the bloodsuckers?"

"Sorry," he says, stomping along the same as before.

It's nearly dark. Remaining on these hills, with all the caves for vampires to hide in, would be sheer foolishness. Especially with Hardin clomping along like he's got rocks tied to his boots.

I pull ahead to join the others and keep my distance from Hardin, which is easy enough, as he hangs back to keep his distance from me.

Taking long strides, Sheriff reaches me and says, "You ain't had nothing to eat in a while, Miss Boswell."

"Gracie," I say.

"Gracie. Have some jerky."

I take the piece she proffers with a *thank you*, and bite into it. Smoky, salty flavors fill my mouth, and my stomach makes a rumble of delight. I finish chewing and say, "This is good."

"Thanks. I smoked it myself." Her voice is full, proud. "My own seasonings and everything."

If I had a little home somewhere, I'd want to play with seasonings. Just a little. Mostly, I think I'd like to sew. I like the feel of different fabrics under my fingers.

But Pa taught me how to cook, and I enjoyed it a fair amount.

"You're a fair good cook," I tell her. "Makes me curious why you decided to become a sheriff."

"A little girl's dream—my dream," she says around her own mouthful of jerky. "I always wanted to help keep law in the land. When the Rift opened, and our little town changed so drastically, I reckon it only strengthened my resolve."

I think on that as we walk. "Nothin' nobler than trying to keep the law."

"Well, isn't that what you do?" she asks.

"Ha! Me? No. A bounty hunter ain't the same at all. I'm mostly in this for the coin. You're in it for the community."

She pops another piece of jerky in her mouth. "You help keep people safe from the outlaws. If that ain't a community-oriented endeavor, I don't know what is." After a pause, she says, "Is it hard being a woman bounty hunter?"

"Some days, I suppose it is. I imagine it's the same being a woman sheriff."

"I imagine you're right. I admire what you do, Gracie Boswell, whether you're in it for the coin or some nobler cause."

Her words make my heart feel a bit bigger in my chest. I didn't know I'd needed someone's praise. Usually, I don't. But getting it free of charge, from a person I respect? It feels mighty good.

Hardin comes right up next to us, ruining my moment. "Mind if I have a piece of that jerky, Sheriff?"

She gives him a grumpy look, but passes a piece to him.

Hardin takes it and makes a loud and obvious sound of enjoyment before stomping away.

I'm about ready to march us all to the Rift and throw this man into its depths.

THIRTEEN

THE NEXT MORNING DAWNS COOL. I wake to the sound of chewing mixing with the sound of a lark's song. Opening my eyes, I sit up and stretch. Sheriff's munching a piece of stale bread. When she sees me watching her, she holds out the other end in offering.

"No, thanks," I say. I don't care to eat first thing in the morning, in general. Like my gut needs a minute to wake up.

My body's still sore from the fae attack yesterday morning, so I rummage in one of my saddlebags and pull out a mending stone. I like to hoard them, save them for when I'm desperate. Today feels like one of those days. I poke one of my fingers on the point of my knife and smear the blood on the stone.

"Mend," I whisper.

It dulls the pain, and I sigh. The world around me looks a lot better now. I can appreciate the colors of the pink and orange sunrise, and the sounds of birdsong.

Hardin gives a loud snore. The man ain't even quiet in his sleep.

Sheriff comes over to sit next to me. "Want to tell me what's wrong?"

Risking a glance at her perceptive gray eyes, I say, "Not particularly."

"Hardin seems to be getting on your last nerve," she says in a low voice.

I look to the man in question. He's asleep with his hat covering his face, his boots off, and brown wool socks sticking out the ends of his trousers. Carson's asleep, too. I swear that man would sleep all day if we let him. Boone and Wesley are sitting a few yards away, breaking their fast with hardtack and jerky.

"He's just loud as anything," I finally say. "I asked him to keep it down and he's still stomping around like he's tryin' to kill a snake."

Sheriff swears in irritation. Boone looks up sharply. I give him a sarcastic wave; we don't need his judgment on what kind of language we use. Just because we're women doesn't mean we can't use colorful epithets from time to time. Instead of appearing angry or annoyed, though, he looks concerned. I shake my head and turn back to the sheriff.

"I can get over it," I say. "Especially if he can start makin' an effort to be quieter."

She sighs. "I feel bad for Mrs. Hardin. She works her fingers to the bone. Hardin's the lucky one in that marriage. I wanted to give him a chance when he offered to help hunt down the outlaws. I hoped he'd surprise me and be useful for a change."

"People surprise me all the time." I run my hand over the scar on my neck, feeling the puckered skin. "Sometimes with their goodness, but oftentimes with their dark sides."

"I reckon you see a lot of that," she says, standing up.

"I wish it weren't so."

Once everyone's up, we saddle the horses to try another hill. I look toward the southwest, in the direction of the grave site. Maybe it wouldn't be so bad to revisit my impulse to free another one of the dead and follow it to its sire. I wonder what Sheriff would have to say about that notion.

As we depart our temporary encampment, Boone hovers close, keeping Pegasus abreast with Kitty. I try slowing Kitty down slightly, then speeding her up slightly, but Boone's constantly there, matching my pace. Feeling ornery, I bring Kitty all the way around Carson's horse and ride in his shadow.

Carson sends me an amused glance. "Tryin' to get away from Boone?"

"Is it that obvious?" I ask.

He chuckles.

"I don't know why he's following me like that," I say, risking a glance at Boone. Instead of looking at me, though, he's looking away, a mean expression on his face. It's hard to imagine that mouth smiling.

"I reckon he likes you," Carson says. "And because he likes you, he's looking out for you."

My face feels extra hot. Hoping Carson can't see it, I say, "The fae attack scared us all."

"Too right it did. I put a piece of hardtack in every

single one of my pockets. I never saw anything like that, Gracie, and I've witnessed some scary scenes in this territory."

Interest piqued, I ask, "What've you seen?"

"Nothing I care to talk about."

The haunted look on his face makes me reluctant to press. The hot sun bakes my plaited hair against my back. I'm grateful for my hat, which blocks a lot of the heat, but I'd love some extra shade. I look up, wishing for clouds, and see some pale wisps so far away, they look more like a prayer for clouds, or the faint idea of clouds, and not real clouds.

I'm rewarded for my patience when Carson continues speaking. "You ever see a demon?"

"Once," I say. "I hope to never have that privilege again."

"Hard for me to agree with that," he says. "The demon I saw was the prettiest thing I ever laid my eyeballs on."

"She?"

"That was the form," he says.

I guess I can't argue whether or not that's possible, as I've only seen one demon. Very few people have seen any, so I haven't heard contrary accounts.

"How are you living to tell this tale?" I ask, unable to keep the skepticism from my voice.

"She weren't there for me," he says.

I suck in a breath. "Someone you knew?"

He tilts his head back and forth. "Extended family. I wasn't close with him. He tried to make a deal to get my ma killed."

"Your ma? That's awful."

"The deal backfired, apparently. I wasn't too sorry to see him dragged away by the demon."

I'm so fascinated by his tale, I almost miss the flash of red in the brush, winking at me like a flapping bird's wing.

"Stop," I whisper, putting the slightest pressure in my hips on Kitty so she halts. I climb off of her, trying not to wince at the dull ache in my back. The mending stone helped, but it ain't nearly as strong as the healing charms around my wrist.

Bending down, I unwrap the red calico from around the branches of the mesquite. The strip of cloth hasn't been out here long, if the brilliant dye and the crisp fabric are any indication. I hold it up for Sheriff to see.

She nods, her face somber. "That would be from the Browning girl's dress."

Hardin nods, also. "I remember she had it on the morning they took off to find their brother."

They came through here, then. Maybe the scrap of fabric was left as a clue, or maybe forgotten during a struggle. I wrap it around my fingers, clenching it like the pressure will squeeze out answers.

We circle around the area, hoping for another piece of red fabric, and we're rewarded when Boone says, "Over here."

"She's leaving us clues," Sheriff says. "Bless that child, she was always a smart one."

"Either that, or the vampires are leaving them on purpose," I grumble.

It's a sobering thought, and we move forward with caution.

We haven't gone much farther when a sour stench fills my nose. It doesn't smell like anything I'd normally find in nature, not even a rotting body. Takes me a minute to figure what it is—bile, human vomit.

It's on the other side of the bushes nearest me. I climb off of Kitty, grab her reins, and lead her along as I follow signs of disturbance in the scraggly vegetation. I'm aware of everyone following behind. I'm grateful, again, that it's more than just me out here. I'd be awful spooked if I was alone, following a trail that leads to what will undoubtedly be the sorry end to a sorry tale.

Pa once told me the dark seems scary because we can't see everything it hides. But to me, the daylight's a lot scarier. I don't want to see what the light has to reveal. Some things are better left secret, unseen.

The trail I've been following—scuffs in the dirt, mostly—becomes dragging marks. Chills race up my spine. I think of holding back, letting someone else move forward ahead of me to discover whatever the scrubby desert is offering up.

Two figures rest under the shade of a tall brittlebush, its yellow flowers at odds with the image of two bloodied men propped against the bushes. One of the men leans back awkwardly, eyes closed, a trickle of blood on his neck. The other stares straight forward, almost as if he's looking through me. Dead? A fly lands on his face and he twitches, although he doesn't brush the insect away.

Boone's at my side all of a sudden, striding forward with purpose. I match his steps. As we get closer, I can see that the man lying down is dead. His chest is still and the blood on his neck is more black than red.

"Hi there," I say to the other. "Can you tell me what happened here?"

No response. I'd expect him to jump up, thank the heavens that help has finally arrived. But he doesn't even make eye contact with me.

Boone's looking around the surrounding brush, on foot. Carson, Wesley, and Hardin are on their horses, weaving between the bushes. Sheriff dismounts and rushes toward the young men.

"Bill, talk to me," she says. "What happened to you and James? Where'd the vampires go? Are Jacob and Ellamae alive?"

The man doesn't respond, just stares forward. He seems to be in some kind of shock, not recognizing anyone, not responding. I never seen anything like it, and I don't like to see it now. Something about that stare reminds me of something dead. Like his body's still alive, but the soul inside has done and took off.

FOURTEEN

"YOU HAVE to tell me what happened," Sheriff says to the man. "Talk to me, Bill."

Bill says nothing. When I look up to check how far the sun has progressed, I see buzzards circling overhead, attracted by the scent of death.

Then Bill's lips begin to move. "Camille Huber, Frank Huber, Scarlet March."

"What? Bill, what are you going on about?" Sheriff asks. "Where's Ellamae? Where's Jacob?"

Still not looking left or right, and seeming to see straight through Sheriff, Bill continues, "Gabriel Colter, Chastity Marrow, Maeve Dutton, Matthew Bentley, Stewart Wilkins, Beatrice Timberman, Jonathan Timberman—"

"Bill, *enough*," Sheriff says.

He goes on with the names, a seemingly endless list.

"What is he doing?" I ask.

"Hell if I know. He's reciting a bunch of names,

people from town." Tears fill the sheriff's eyes. She dashes them away with her knuckles. "Wesley!"

"Yes, Sheriff," he says, hurrying over and dismounting from his gelding.

"I need you to take Bill home to his ma."

Meanwhile, Bill is still whispering those names.

Wesley frowns. "But, Sheriff—"

"No arguments," she says sharply. "That was our agreement."

That tone of hers strikes me. His eyes are brown whereas hers are gray. His chin is square while hers is rounded. Hell, even the shapes of their hands are different. It's that maternal tone that gives it away—Wesley is her son.

Boone, Carson, and Hardin join us; they didn't find anything else of interest or alarm in the immediate environs. My hand hovers over my holster, though, ready for danger.

Sheriff tries to lift Bill, but can't. Wesley and Hardin try, and they can't do it either. My mending stone didn't heal all of me, and with my aching back and scrambled joints, I know I'll be of little use. I look at Boone and tilt my head. Nodding, he dismounts and comes over. He puts his hands under Bill's arms, like Bill's no more'n a toddler, and brings Bill to his feet.

I half expect Bill to crumple, but he simply stands there like a man who stepped out of his house one morning and forgot where he was planning to go. It's eerie how he don't move or look at anything.

He stops whispering the names, though. He screams once, long and loud.

"What the devil?" Hardin shouts, leaping away from him.

Then Bill says in a guttural voice, "We'll take our bounty in blood. In this land, you're the outlaws."

And then, finally, Bill goes blessedly silent again.

Boone and Wesley work together to get Bill onto Wesley's saddle, then Wesley climbs on behind him. Bill stares stock straight ahead and I fight the shivers.

"Was that a spell causing him to do all that?" Carson asks, looking at me and Boone.

I shrug. "I think so. It sounded like a message."

"Vampires can manipulate dreams with magic," Boone says, "same as any other outlaw or charmslinger. And Bill here looks to be in a waking nightmare."

Hardin scowls and kicks a rock. "I don't like it. I'd like to burn every outlaw and charmslinger right here, right now."

"Enough, Hardin," Sheriff says, her lips thin. "Wesley. You know how to get yourself home?"

Wesley looks to his ma and says, "Yes'm. But Sheriff..."

"Take Bill to a doctor," she says. "And a witch. Both. The gold can come from my safe if his ma can't pay it. And you be careful getting home, you hear?"

"I will," he says. "You, too. Pa can't take another shock."

She nods grimly. "You give my love to your pa."

He tips his hat and then he's riding off, winding his way through the maze of sagebrush and over to the tree-scattered base of the foothills.

I look up. It's closing in around midday, and the sun

is high. More buzzards have joined the others on their circuit overhead.

"We need to bury him," Sheriff says, following my gaze.

"Yep," I say, even though really, *need* ain't a part of this. She *wants* to bury him, and that's a different notion than needing to. "You knew this man?"

"I did."

"Then you might not want to be a part of what I have to do next."

"Why not?" she asks.

Boone speaks up. "Because we need to take his head off. Can't risk him rising."

"We don't do that in Penance," Sheriff says. "We bury them with a second cross, keeps 'em from rising."

"That ain't good enough," I say. "Wooden crosses are temporary. They rot, they get ripped from the ground in a tornado."

"Yeah," Carson says. "A vampire can come along and yank them from the ground. Or anyone could do that, even. Don't have to be a vampire."

I send him a look of irritation, but he just smiles widely, showing off his pretty lips and straight teeth.

"Not only that," I add, "anyone with a half-decent necromancy charm can bring a body back if it has a head. You don't want a body brought back after it's been bit by a bloodsucker."

"We should have thought of that," Sheriff says.

"Most towns don't think of it," I tell her. "Anyway, there's a spade in one of Kitty's bags. It's small, but it'll have to do. If you want, you can start digging the grave while we take care of the body."

Nodding, she goes for the saddlebags. Her shoulders are tight with tension. Hardin goes with her, his steps reluctant.

Boone, Carson, and I face the body.

"I have a spade, too," Carson says quickly. "I'll help the sheriff."

He hurries after Sheriff and Hardin.

"Our pup doesn't much like blood, I think," Boone says in a none-too-quiet voice, although I'm standing right next to him.

"Maybe you like blood a little too much," Carson calls as he opens one of his saddlebags and pulls out a spade like mine. Carrying one is dead useful.

"Just your blood," Boone says, hand resting on his pistol.

Carson sneers. "Don't make me hex you."

"You two done yet?" I ask.

"Suppose so," Boone says.

Boone straightens the body in front of us while I pull my knife from its sheath.

"It ain't none of my business," I say to Boone as I take stock of the man's neck. This isn't going to be pretty. I'm glad the sheriff has agreed to be otherwise occupied. "But I do wonder why you and Carson seem to be at odds. Do you not trust him?"

"I trust him well enough," Boone says over the sound of spades scraping against the dirt. "I reckon he just makes me ornery sometimes."

The dead man's skin is warm in the heat of the day,

almost like he's living. Shivers run up and down my spine and I roll my shoulders, trying to shake them off.

"You want me to do it?" Boone asks, quiet enough not to call attention to my hesitation.

"Nah, I got it," I say, and get to work, trying not to think too hard about what I'm doing. Vampire, human, whatever creature it is, the head doesn't want to come off the neck. It fights the knife every time. And I don't blame it. My body wouldn't be too eager to part with my head, either.

Boone takes over when I sit back to rest. He rolls up his shirtsleeves, revealing tanned forearms corded with muscle. On his wrist is a leather wrap with tiny bone beads sewn onto it in a zigzag pattern. There's got to be at least a hundred beads on there.

"That's a nice-looking charm," I say.

"It is indeed."

It must've cost him a lot of gold, that much time went into its creation. The cheaper the charm, the less effort into its craft. The charms that go in my pistol are nothing more than spelled rocks, far as I know. The charmed bracelets on my wrist, though—they're formed with polished stones that have been turned into beads, then carefully strung on knotted twine.

Time and intent create more powerful magic. Looks like a witch sat with Boone's bracelet for days. I reckon it won't just save him from having one foot in the grave, but dig him right out if he happens to go all the way in.

The sun's past overhead, moving into the west, by the time the grave is dug, and the sky is fairly speckled with buzzards. Carson, Hardin, and Sheriff step back, spades held loosely at their sides.

"It's not deep," Sheriff says, "but it'll do."

I look down at the corpse. Boone rested the head against the shoulder. I think he means it as a sign of respect to keep it close to the neck where it used to belong, but it looks grotesque, like some kind of joke, a man leaning his head on his own shoulder. I have to fight the urge to look away in disgust.

Covering up the body would be preferable, but spare cloth is in short supply in this wasteland of a desert prairie. Eyes locked on the corpse's head, I imagine fangs protruding, lips pulled back in a sneer, dark eyes flashing with triumph as another soul bleeds into the earth.

I want to burn the head, too, even though I know it's an unnecessary superstition. Rubbing the chills from my arms, I look away.

We lower the body and head into the grave and bury the man. Spadefuls of dirt make swishing sounds as they land on him. Sheriff says a few words. Hardin says a few words. I don't like how far the sun has gone toward the west. We've lost time—too much time. I rock back and forth on my boot heels, trying to keep a low profile, but inside I'm grinding my teeth together and wishing for a swift end to this impromptu ceremony.

Once it's done, I walk straight over to Kitty and climb into the saddle. Carson, Hardin, and the sheriff follow suit, and Boone takes a last look at the freshly turned earth of the grave before joining us.

Something's been niggling in the back of my mind. Something about what Bill said.

"Sheriff," I say, "what were those names Bill recited? Friends of his?"

"Townspeople of Penance," she says.

"Ah, all right, then. Maybe he's homesick."

She shakes her head. "Doubtful. Those are all people the vamps killed."

"Every one of them that he said?" I ask. "No extras?"

"No extras."

Earlier, Carson mentioned how anyone could pull out the second crosses from the graves. And Bill just recited all the names of the dead. He was doing it for a reason, and I have an inkling as to what that reason was.

I don't wait to explain. We need to get to that grave site and we need to do it now. I nudge Kitty southwest at a gallop. The others fall in behind me, Carson shouting, "What are you doing, Gracie?"

"The grave site," I say, looking over my shoulder at him. "I need to make sure it's intact."

I catch a glimpse of his face, slack with shock, before I turn forward in my saddle again.

The sun is setting. We wasted too much time on that grave for Bill's brother. I knew it. Time spent on compassion during a crisis is time wasted, whether or not it separates us from the monsters. In cases like this, it's compassion that can get us eaten.

"Don't you think you're overreacting?" Hardin calls over the galloping hoofbeats.

"I sure hope I am," I shout over my shoulder.

I'm sure everything's fine. Nothing would please me more than to find everything in its place and figure that Bill was reciting those names because of the tragedy, that's all. It don't have nothing to do with their graves. We'll get there and see everything as I left it after pulling up that one cross.

We reach the slight rise of a hill, then follow the dip down to where that narrow creek separates the graves from the fastest route to Penance. The sun has gone down.

Tossing a piece of hardtack in the creek, I feel my heart sink into my stomach as I survey the land before me.

Thirty-four crosses lay on the ground, ripped from the earth and scattered like splintered branches ravaged by a storm.

Now I understand what Bill was saying for the vampires—not the names, but that other part he said. A blood bounty. They'll take their bounty in blood. In freeing a small army, they've turned the tables and made us not the bounty hunters, but the hunted.

FIFTEEN

IT'S DUSK, barely light enough for a human to see without a charm. Sheriff makes a sound of dismay at the sight of the crosses littered over the ground.

"We're going to see seventeen new vampires rise tonight, aren't we?" she says in a soft voice.

I don't respond, because she knows just as well as I do.

"Sixteen," Carson says, unhelpfully. "Gracie set one free a couple nights ago so we could follow it."

"You did?" Sheriff asks.

"I did, and I apologize for any slight to you or the people of Penance. I don't apologize for the tactic." I can be compassionate but stand by my strategy.

She nods absently, her eyes on the grave mounds in front of us. The dirt isn't disturbed yet, other than almost invisible holes where the crosses used to punch into the earth.

"I say we leave one to run, stake the rest." I climb off of Kitty. "Surround the area, come at 'em from all sides—"

"No time for planning," Boone says, starting forward. "They're rising now."

He's right. A single hand juts up from the dirt, fingers splayed like it's hoping for another hand to grasp.

Rift take Boone, he's galloping toward the graves, his pistol raised in the air. Is this why he got all those bounties out from under me? The man doesn't hesitate. I urge Kitty forward and she's nearly as fast as Pegasus. Wind whips my face as we rush to the graves.

Pounding hooves is my only clue the others are behind me. No one shouts, no one says a word. We surge forward like a rushing river.

Boone's on the first bloodsucker as it rises, stunning it with an arc of green light from his pistol. More are rising. I raise my pistol and take aim, accounting for the rolling of Kitty's motion.

The charm blasts from my pistol, shooting outward across the graves to where it lands harmlessly at the base of a tree stump. Swearing under my breath, I take aim once more.

Sixteen vampires rising, five of us. The math ain't reassuring. Our only saving grace is the outlaws who freed these vamps are nowhere around, as there's nowhere for them to hide. They must've come upon these graves last night, just before sunrise, when it was too close to dawn for the new vampires to wake.

Sixteen vampires, down to fifteen now that Boone's jumped off Pegasus to stake the vampire he stunned.

"Leave one alive," I shout, not bothering to debate with myself on whether any of them could actually be considered "living." Regardless, we need someone to follow when this is done. It'll go after its sire, and with all five of us humans following it, we won't be surprised with any counterattacks this time.

Arcs of green light flash as Boone, Carson, and I shoot charms. I hear the loud pops and the whizzing noise of metal bullets, too, which makes me want to duck my head. But this ain't no time to cower.

The stunner charms and bullets don't kill the vampires, it's the stakes that'll do that, so when I see a vampire go down from a charm or a bullet, I take one of the stakes from my thigh sheath and hurl it at the fallen body. The charm on the stake helps it fly true and strong. One after another, the vampires fall, their blood spattering the ground, black like tar.

Everything's surprisingly quiet. The vampires don't scream, and we don't holler at 'em as we put on our own attack and dodge theirs. The entire battle is concentration and silent strength, a restrained bloodbath.

My head begins to ache at the magic I'm using, but I fight through it like I always do.

Hardin either fell off of his horse, or jumped off. Standing on the ground, he's got a vampire in front of him, its arms curving forward. Any second now and the outlaw will rush Hardin. I don't think his chances are good, despite the stake he holds. He looks like he don't know how to find the pointy part, even.

Nobody else is watching him—they all have their own opponents. Sighing, I wheel Kitty around and we gallop to Hardin and his vampire. Hearing us, the vampire turns and looks up.

Now, I think at Hardin. *Now, stake it now.*

Hardin doesn't do a thing.

My pistol's out of bullets, so I pull my last stake from its sheath. The night feels cold and clear against my cheeks and I can feel my braid whipping behind me as Kitty and I charge the vampire. It spins fully to face us, its cruel mouth twisted with murderous intent.

I'm about to hurl the stake into its chest when Boone shouts, "Boswell! That's the last one!"

Curling my fingers tighter around the stake, I hold it close instead of sending it to its target.

Hardin lunges at the vampire.

"Let it go," I shout.

It's as if he didn't hear me—he attacks the vampire from the back, stabbing it with the stake. The vamp's mouth opens in a twist of pained surprise, and it falls forward, face in the dirt of a broken grave.

SIXTEEN

"I TOLD you to let it go!" I scream at Hardin.

He flashes me an obstinate look and yanks his stake from the vampire's back. "You said no prisoners."

"Yes, I said that," I agree, rubbing my temples, "but then I said let this one go. We were going to follow it to its sire, you fool."

"Call me a fool again," he says, standing up tall as he can.

"Rift take you," I say, "I've had enough of this. Sheriff, send him home. This man is more of a hindrance than a help."

Sheriff's picking her hat up off the ground and turning fallen vampire bodies over so as she can see their faces and retrieve our stakes. A wave of sorry, bitter and sour at the same time, rolls through me at the thought that some of these vampires might've once been people she called friends.

"I apologize," Hardin says, slumping his shoulders as

Sheriff reaches him. "Don't send me back, I want to help."

She stands before him, hands on her hips, her gray eyes looking silver in the moonlight. "You want to stay, then you will listen to and respect Miss Boswell."

He nods. "Yes'm."

Sighing, Sheriff clicks her tongue and her horse ambles over, shying away from the slain vampires.

"We don't have time to bury sixteen people all over again, do we?" she says to me.

"I reckon we don't," I say. My head aches like a giant's squeezing it between its thumb and forefinger. "Not unless we want to be burying sixteen more over the course of the week."

She nods and looks over the carnage. Some of the faces, and the tar-like blood, could make a stomach turn, but she merely nods, one hand on her hip, the other hand on her horse's mane.

"Any idea why someone would purposefully remove all these crosses?" she asks.

"The vampires have a plan," Boone says.

Sheriff turns back to look at us, surprise in her eyes. "A plan?"

"Yes'm," I say. "They mean to take Penance, make it their own. They said as much when Boone, Carson, and I first hunted 'em down. Freeing your dead townspeople was just one way for them to increase their numbers."

"I never heard of bloodsuckers taking on a goal like this," she mutters. "I should've moved out of Penance as soon as I was old enough to shoot a gun. Damned Rift town."

I let her mutter to herself for a moment, then clear my throat and look pointedly at the slain vampires. Sheriff sighs.

"Vampires burn fairly easy, don't they?" she asks.

"They do," Carson says.

Sheriff sighs again, as if steeling herself for a tough job. "Is it as good as removing their heads?"

"Yes'm," Boone says. "Faster, too, when there's this many of 'em."

She bends at the waist and grabs the hands of one of the vampires, dragging it to the center of the graves. There, she lets it go and grabs another. I climb off of Kitty to help her, and the men help as well, hauling bodies into a pile.

"You all right, Sheriff?" I ask.

She nods once, her movement restrained. "I already said farewell to these folks once. Seemed like enough of a goodbye at the time."

It's similar to what happened with Pa. I hadn't even finished mourning him before he died all over again.

She reaches into her saddlebag and finds a box of matches. After lighting one, she tosses it on the pile of vampires. At first I think the flame isn't going to catch, but then the entire pile lights up in a *whoosh* of fire.

My head aches. Sheriff looks thoughtful as she watches the flames. I bet she's thinking of the vampire nest that wants to make its home in her town.

As I watch Sheriff watch the vampires burn, a winking reflection catches my eye. I stare harder past Sheriff and into the shadowed hills.

"What d'you see?" Carson asks, coming up at my side.

"It's a house I saw last time we were here. There's a light on."

Boone walks up to my other side. "We might could take some refuge tonight."

Before I can even part my lips to warn we should practice caution, Sheriff and Carson agree. Hardin, too. They mount their horses and are riding toward the house before I even reach Kitty.

Who's in charge of this posse, anyway? Sure as hell don't seem to be me.

———

THE HOUSE IS a big ranch house, two stories tall. It's occupied, as a lantern burns, lighting up one of the windows. We ride to the front and dismount. Anyone awake inside would've heard us ride up, so Boone calls out, "Hello. We're bounty hunters, just looking for a place to shelter for the night."

"We don't want to cause any inconvenience," Sheriff adds.

The door opens and orange-yellow lamplight streams over the wooden planks of the wide front porch. An older woman stands in front of us. She's fully dressed, and still wearing her apron.

"I've cooked supper," she says. "And there's enough to share. Come in, come in."

The scent of cooking meat and vegetables fills my nostrils. Delicious.

But something ain't right. It's the way her head cocks to the side, the way her skin glows.

She's a fae, wearing a glamour.

Hardin starts forward, fast as anything. I stop him with a hand out. "All is not as it seems," I say to him. "Don't agree to nothing she suggests."

Boone murmurs something under his breath, agreeing with me.

Hardin glances from me to Boone.

"I won't harm you," the fae says, her voice old and sweet.

Could be she's telling the truth. Not all fae are dangerous. Some are just trying to get along with humans and live regular lives.

To gauge whether or not she's on our side, I ask, "Do you know anything about a nest of vampires in these hills?"

"Not in these hills," she says with a shake of her head. The wrinkles around her eyes crinkle as she smiles at us. "They went west."

"When?" I ask.

"I'll tell you all about it over supper," she says. "There's room in the barn for your horses, and extra feed. You folks look like you can use a rest."

If she hadn't tried to convince us, I might've believed her. But she's working a little too hard to get us to settle in with her. Not that I'd have spent the night here for anything. Just whatever she has cooking smells heavenly.

Frowning at us, she says, "You wouldn't say no to a nice, hot supper, would you?"

"You're a fae," Boone says. "What is it you really want with us?"

"A fae?" Hardin spits on the ground.

Her bright eyes glow briefly, the glamour flickering before settling over her again. "I'm a harmless grandmother—"

Hardin's face is a mask of revulsion and loathing as he stares at the fae. He lifts his gun, arm shaking slightly.

"No!" I shout.

He shoots.

Damn him to the Rift. He's ignored just about every order I've given him.

She falls to the ground, her arms bent awkwardly under her body.

"I hope that bullet was iron," Carson says, "or she's going to jump up in a second, and she isn't going to go down quite so easy a second time."

I shudder, remembering the glamourless forms of the fae I've battled.

When Hardin doesn't respond, Boone says, "Iron or lead? Which did you use?"

Lead shoots straighter, but all it does is enrage outlaws. Iron will stop a fae or a witch. It'll slow down a demon, some say, but there's not much research in that arena. Nobody knows its effect on shapeshifters. Silver is most often used for them, but as I've never taken a shapeshifter bounty, I wouldn't know. And I don't shoot bullets, anyhow.

"It's iron," Hardin says. "I'm no fool."

"That's debatable," Carson says, but he starts toward the fallen fae.

I follow right behind him. As we get closer to the door of the house, the savory scent of the fae's cooking causes my mouth to water.

"You reckon we can steal some of that supper?" Carson asks as he nudges the fae over with his boot.

A hole goes through her forehead. Her glamour's fading now that she's dead, her skin tingeing to a pale, pale white—almost silver. Her gray and white old woman hair thickens and becomes green. A salty, oily scent rises from her body.

Hardin comes up to survey the corpse.

"You shouldn't have killed her like that," I say to him. "She wasn't provoking us."

"She was trying to tempt us into her house," he says. "I've heard about fae invitations."

He's not wrong. Still, we could've climbed back on our horses and ridden away.

"What about that supper?" Carson asks.

I send him a hard look. "Do you think with anything except your stomach?"

"It's not like she's going to eat it now," he says.

Shaking my head, I say, "Fine, we can go in. Keep an eye out, though. Most fae live alone unless they're breeding. We search the whole house before even entertaining the idea of eating."

Hardin and Boone search upstairs. Carson, Sheriff, and I search downstairs.

"You reckon she was speaking the truth about the bloodsuckers?" Sheriff asks.

"No way to know," I say, glaring at the ceiling where I hear Hardin's boots stomping around. "She's dead so I can't ask. Fae can be tricky, though. I doubt she'd have given us that information for free, so I'm having a hard time trusting it."

Sheriff nods. "I'm thinking the same."

The delicious scent is coming from a pot of stew on the hearth. Once we determine the downstairs clear, Carson reaches for the pot.

"Not yet," I say. "Wait for the others. We don't want to have accepted her invitation and be obliged to someone else in her stead."

Fae rules are more complicated than demons'. Contracts with demons are straightforward. They rarely go well for humans because we just aren't smart enough to rule out all the possible exclusions and inclusions. Fae, however, will entreat you to enter into all manner of unspoken contracts, the navigation of which is murky, especially to humans. Those contracts often revolve around favors and offerings.

"It's clear up there," Boone says, descending a set of rickety, narrow stairs. "A family used to live here. It ain't dusty at all. They were recently killed, I suspect."

I sigh. Homes like this, out in the middle of nowhere, are easy pickings for the outlaws.

The table is set for two. I walk over to it, run a finger over one of the smooth porcelain dishes. Must've been expensive to get these bowls all the way out west. When I lift my finger, it comes up clean—not a speck of dust.

"Maybe the fae just killed them today," I say. "Maybe that was supposed to be their supper."

Hardin ambles over to the hearth. Lifting the ladle from the pot, he blows on it. The scent of onions and pepper reaches my nose and my stomach growls. Putting his lips to the ladle, Hardin has a taste.

"It's real good," he says. "I'll have to check the spice cupboard, see if there's anything to bring back for the missus so she can make this, too. Pass me a bowl?"

Carson hands him one, and Hardin spills a ladleful of stew into the bowl.

Boone backs up, shaking his head, eyes wide. "No."

He's staring right at the bowl. I'm shorter than he is, so the angle is wrong for me to see inside of it. Doesn't matter what I can or can't see, because Hardin drops the bowl on the floor. Stew splashes out and the porcelain breaks.

A finger.

There's a human finger, flesh still on it, lying in a puddle of the stew.

Hardin spins around, braces himself on the wall, and vomits. Sheriff gags, too. My stomach roils and I swallow several times, trying to keep the gagging at bay.

Boone's hand is warm on my elbow as he leads me from the farmhouse. The others are on our heels. We hurry past the fallen fae and climb onto our horses. I lean forward, breathing in Kitty's dusty coat, trying to forget the scent of the stew in that kitchen.

SEVENTEEN

WE ENDED up sleeping about five miles from the farm-house. The scent of stew permeated our clothes. I found an old well and dumped the stagnant water over myself, preferring that stink to the savory one that followed me.

Back at the foothills, we continue to search for the vampire nest.

Tempers are short. Boone's mad we ain't following the fae's advice and heading west. He says there ain't no reason not to trust her. "Just 'cause she's an outlaw don't mean she's lyin'."

I say there ain't no reason to trust her. Until we've turned over every rock in these hills, I'm not going west.

As we search, I snap at Hardin more than once, and even Sheriff looks like she's apt to strangle him if he don't quiet his footsteps.

"Last night," Hardin mutters, "I finally saw the true face of evil. Brought here by the outlaws."

"Evil was here before the outlaws," I say.

"What do you mean?" Carson asks.

"There's always been evil in this territory," I say. "Even before the Rift. What do you call the decimation of entire nations so we could steal their land?"

Nobody answers me. Hardin's hazel eyes grow big in alarm.

I continue, "Exactly. So the Rift? The outlaws? They just made evil more obvious to the white folk."

I have to get away from all of these people before I shove them all down the side of the hill.

Keeping my eyes wide open for vampires or a sign of their nest, I maneuver past a little copse of juniper trees and over a piece of sunbaked granite large enough for me to walk on. A portion of it juts up at chest-height. I thought there could be a hollow back here, but I thought wrong. Irritated, I turn to go. My boots scuff against some loose dirt against the rock, and the granite ledge tilts as I slip. Throwing out a hand, I grab the ledge.

Saved.

Until I hear the unmistakable sound of a rattler.

I jerk my hand back, but not in time. The snake strikes and its fangs puncture my skin. I give a muffled yelp in alarm and follow it up with a curse for being so foolish. Snake-bit *and* loud about it.

"Boswell!" Boone comes around the ledge, sees me holding my hand and the tail of the snake disappearing into the shadows behind the granite ledge.

"Mending stones are in my saddlebag," I say, sliding down to sit on the ground. And the saddlebag is the way at the bottom of the hill, with Kitty. That was mighty foolish of me.

He crouches next to me. Taking my hand in his, he

examines the wound. He glances down the steep slope of the hill. He raises his eyebrows, as if reading my mind. "I've a couple in my pocket. Just a second."

I try to tug my hand away from his, but he doesn't let go as he fishes in his pocket with his other hand.

"You're mad at me for not listening to the fae's advice," I say. "Why're you helping me?"

"Why're you being silly?" he asks, keeping hold of my hand.

I purse my lips, feeling ornery. Finally, I say, "She had no reason to tell us anything for free."

"Unless she just wanted to help."

"Out of the goodness of her heart?" I snort. "Doubtful."

"You might be surprised, Boswell," he says as he wipes a stone against the blood on the back of my hand. He invokes the magic with a muttered, "Heal."

"I don't want to take another one of your mending stones." I try to pull out of his grasp, but he ain't having it. "I have my own."

"You have a streak of stubbornness deeper than the Rift is what you have," he says.

Well, that's unfair. "I ain't stubborn."

Fire burns through my hand, traveling up to my elbow. Boone lets me go when I try one more time to get out of his reach.

"You ain't stubborn? Then take the stone." He holds it up. It glimmers innocently in the afternoon light.

I could make it down the hill and to the mending stones in my saddlebag before the venom causes permanent damage or death. Or I could take Boone's stone.

"Fine," I say, reaching for it.

He grabs my hand again and slides the stone against my palm. The relief is immediate and I feel my shoulders sag down as the tension in my body melts away.

"I don't think the vampires are on this hill," I say as the burning pain subsides. "We would've found them by now. They're long gone, to some better hideout while they get ready to take over the town."

His warm palm continues to hold mine. It feels strangely intimate and I'm not sure how to take my hand back without calling attention to the moment. It ain't entirely unpleasant, if I'm being honest. And when he flicks his caramel gaze up to meet mine, my breath stutters in my chest.

"You all right?" he asks softly.

I nod, unable to look away from the softness in his eyes. A scruff has grown on his chin and cheeks, making him look more rugged. I've a sudden urge to feel it against my palm.

Once again, it's as if the man can read my mind, because he pulls on my wrist and presses my hand to his face, his eyes never leaving mine. I barely register the scratchy texture of his cheek before he brushes his lips against my skin. My breath hitches in my throat and I feel warm all over.

He gives me a soft smile, then stands and pulls me up, too.

"Gracie? Boone?" Carson's voice is faint as it winds through the copse of junipers.

"Back here, we're coming," I say, pulling away from Boone and hurrying forward.

We reach the others, who are on their way down the hill. Sheriff's cursing up a storm.

"What's the problem?" I ask.

She shakes her head. "Every little cave we've found has been no more'n a divot in the rock. Hardly a place for vampires to hide."

"You don't have any other large caverns in these parts?" I ask her.

She shakes her head. "Not that I recall."

The vampires aren't here. Maybe that fae was telling us the truth, after all. "We have to go west."

"Like the fae said?" Hardin says. "Hell if I'm going to listen to any damned fae."

Everyone else ignores him. Boone's light brown eyes are intent on mine. "You think we should do what the fae suggested, Boswell?"

"I don't like it. The bloodsuckers were in these hills when we got here, but we've searched all over and they're nowhere to be seen. Maybe she was being honest."

He nods. "And at no gain to herself. She didn't even barter for that information. Almost as if she did it out of the goodness of her heart."

I ignore his unspoken censure. "There was more to it than that," I say.

Grinning, he says, "Oh, I believe she fully intended to add one of us to her stew. But I also believe she gave us the information on the vampires for free."

Hardin looks a little green in the face at the mention of the stew.

"We need to rest before we go anywhere," Carson says.

I look over at him. He looks awake and strong as always. "Don't be lazy."

"I ain't," he says with a growl to his voice, then cocks his head toward Hardin. "We're all about to fall off our horses with fatigue. We've been going all day."

"Fine," I say, my voice sharp. "Let's ride west and find a place to make camp."

We get on our horses and ride. I'm stewing inside. The vampires don't seem to be anywhere around when we want to find them. But they're everywhere when we don't. They've killed one of the Brownings. They've caused an entire grave site to erupt with new vampires.

I allow Kitty's soft movements to lull me and I fall into thought. A voice fills my mind. It ain't real, not like the vampire's voice that one night, coming at us through unseen places in the darkness. But it's similar in how it can't be stopped. *You'll fail, Gracie. Everyone's going to suffer.* As it speaks, over and over again I see my father's face change.

That night when I was fourteen, I woke up from what I'd hoped was a nightmare to see him standing there in the cabin in front of me. He was alive. Everything with the vampire the night before, it was just a bad dream. And then Pa was there, standing over my bed.

Vampires don't return to their homes. They don't like reminders of their humanity. They'd rather find their sires and form a nest. Even as a girl, I knew these things.

But Pa's sire was dead—I killed it the night before. He couldn't go searching for it, because it was gone. And we lived far away from any town. The nearest homestead was miles and miles away.

Pa wasn't alive—he'd risen as a vampire.

And he was thirsty.

Because of the vampire attack and Pa's death the night before, I'd felt unsafe going to sleep. There was a stake under my pillow. I'd spent all day whittling it, in between my other household chores. I knew I couldn't stay there on the little homestead on my own, but I didn't know where else to go. I'd never slung a charm. I'd never even met a witch.

Pa stood over me, and his eyes showed no recognition of his daughter. He hissed, pulled his lips back, reached for me.

"Pa?" I said, my voice small and hoarse from sleep.

The way he reached for me almost seemed like a hug, and I reached for him too. But my hand was still on the stake under my pillow. It took only a second for my sleep-fogged brain to figure out what was going on. Then his teeth were in my neck and I was screaming.

The stake. I knew I had to use it. Wasn't no question in my head about that. There was a different question, though—was I strong enough to kill my own pa?

Turned out I was, or I wouldn't be riding Kitty through this outlaw-infested territory.

I don't want to think about Pa anymore. I cried for him for weeks and weeks, months and months. Hell, I cry for him still. Probably always will. He was both my pa and my ma. He was my whole family.

And this vampire nest wants to ruin all the families in an entire Rift town. I think about the stable girl in Penance, held in a dark room, waiting for the fanged creature of night. I think about Hardin's wife and son. Sheriff and Wesley, and Sheriff's husband. Minerva Browning and her remaining children.

I think about that beautiful, sparkling city coming under shadow.

"Silver," I say. "Penance is the silver city."

Boone, Carson, and Sheriff all turn to look at me like I've lost my mind. Hardin continues on, oblivious.

I halt Kitty and stare back at the sheriff, at her silver eyes, her silver belt buckle, her silver earrings.

I say, *"Where are the mines?"*

EIGHTEEN

SHERIFF'S HORSE steps a little closer to me and Kitty so we can see each other better. Her voice is stern, but her eyes keen with curiosity. "I'm not exactly grasping what you're getting at."

"There have to be mines, surely?" I say. "I saw the sign when I rode in. *Penance: The City of Silver.*"

"That's right," Sheriff says slowly. She still ain't certain where I'm going with this. "But since the Rift, we don't mine it anymore."

"So where are the mines at?"

She taps her chin. "You know, I don't rightly know. They stopped using them when I was girl. It's too damn close to the Rift."

It's too damn close to the Rift, I repeat in my mind. I don't like it, but this was never a journey for pleasure. The vampires take away everything good in the world. Families torn apart the same way they tear necks in their search for blood.

After Pa died, I vowed to do whatever I could to get rid of them.

But I never thought my mission would send me this close to the Rift.

A cold wash of fear slides over my body, but I keep my face straight. "We need to find the mines. If they're gathering an army of bloodsuckers, that'll be where they'll do it. Biggest possible place for them to hide."

"The mines are all closed up," Hardin says. "It ain't worth it to go all the way up there."

"You think bloodsuckers are going to care about a sign saying something is closed and dangerous?" I ask, nudging Kitty forward.

"Where you going, Boswell?" Boone asks, his voice low.

"I'm going to the mountains. The vampires are in the mines. You all can come, or you can stay behind, I don't much care."

He pulls up alongside of me. "How do you know they're in the mines?"

"I just do. It's where I'd keep a large nest." I have a job to do, and I don't look behind to see if the group is following. I can't let the vampires win. I can't let them take over Penance, ruin other families like they ruined mine.

The sound of horses' hooves alerts me to the fact that the others are following despite my less than warm invitation.

"This is going to be even more dangerous than I thought," I say to them. "You can stay back. No one's a coward in a situation like this."

I peek over my shoulder. Hardin looks like he's giving my words great consideration. Carson don't even blink, and neither does the sheriff.

"I don't think we'll even find them there," Hardin says, "but we'll surely find worse creatures that close to the Rift."

"Don't know what you mean by worse," I say, "when this nest's goal is to move into your city and turn you all into walking goblets of blood."

He's quiet after that, but I can sense his resistance.

Turning to the sheriff, I say, "What's the fastest way to the mines, or to wherever it is you think the mines are most likely to be?"

She jerks her chin west. "We loop around Penance and we'll come to a valley. We get in there, travel northwest for a couple of miles, and I think we'll find it."

It takes us a few hours to reach the valley, and when we finally arrive, it's full dark. I debate continuing on to the mines regardless of our lack of sunlight. However, I'd rather all five of us are alert and rested as well as possible before heading into any tunnels tomorrow.

There ain't nothing around us, no stream, just scrubby juniper no taller than my head. I don't know about the others, but my canteen is only partly full. The horses had a drink sometime after noon, but they must be thirsty after riding through the late afternoon and evening. I don't like not knowing the country I'm traveling in or where the next drink is coming from.

"We'll rest here, I suppose," I say. "I wish there was some water, though."

Boone speaks up. "If we go another mile or so, we should reach a well."

"You know this area?" Sheriff asks.

"It's the one I pointed to on the map you sketched for us," Boone says. "I've been out here before."

"Do I know you?" Sheriff asks.

"No, ma'am, I don't think so," he says.

"If you lived around here or came out here before, maybe our paths crossed," she says.

He looks uncomfortable. "I don't believe they did."

I allow Boone to lead the way and I'm surprised when he stops in the middle of nothing. It's just more scrub and dirt as far as I can tell in the moonlight.

"Here's the well," he says, climbing off Pegasus's saddle and standing next to a low, rock-lined hole.

His eyes are pinched with some emotion I can't place as he lifts a long cord of rope and tests its durability by stretching it tight. Nodding, he checks the knot on a pail, then lowers it into the hole. A faint splash echoes against the rocks.

"There's still water." He tosses down a piece of hardtack before dragging the pail back up. He takes a sip from the pail, nods. "Still good. It's fed by an underground stream coming from the mountains."

Everyone takes care of their horses and grabs bedrolls.

Boone's movements are a little jerkier than usual. He usually moves smoothly, like flowing water over river rocks, but now there's a barely concealed rage as he unfolds his bedroll and places it on the ground.

"Boone, you all right?" I ask him.

"Just need a minute," he says, then walks off into the darkness.

Sheriff and Carson claim my ears with a debate on the merits of hardtack over smoked jerky. Hardin's sulking off to the side, and I wonder why he didn't just ride back home. No shame in it if he don't agree with the course of our hunt. I wouldn't blame him. He's just a barkeep, he didn't sign up for a ride to the Rift.

Neither did I, but I'm going to see this through.

Carson says, "Hardtack tastes like wood."

"Yes," Sheriff says with practiced patience, "but jerky sucks all the moisture out of a person. Tastes good, sure, if you don't mind dying of thirst after you've had a bite."

I sit on my bedroll, ready to take my sleep while the other two keep watch, seein' as how they're lively enough to stay awake a couple hours. But I see Boone wandering around the scrub. Doesn't look like he's searching for a place to piss, because any of these bushes would do.

He's looking for something.

I don't know if it's curiosity or concern that motivates me to stand up and make my way toward him. He looks up at my approach, an irritated glance that he returns to the ground at his feet.

"I said I need a minute," he says.

"Your pacing is wearing a rift into the earth," I say. "What are you doing out here?"

"Pacing," he says shortly.

Well, that would be obvious to a dead man. "You seem like you're looking for something."

He doesn't speak, so I cast my gaze around. Thanks to my sight charm, I can make out enough to distinguish scrub brush from dirt, and that's when I notice some weathered boards near my feet. They're not much more'n splinters.

"There was a house here once, that went with the well," I say carefully.

He looks up. "Yes, there was."

I walk along the boards to make out the shape of the house. "You ain't looking for the house."

"No."

I can guess where the door would've been, but I don't know for sure. No way to know. I imagine if I had a little home out in the middle of a valley, I'd want the kitchen window facing east, so's I could prepare breakfast while watching the sunrise over the mountains. This pretty little valley would make for a delightful sunrise and sunset. I run the toe of my boot along the dirt, daydreaming. I'd have the front door about here.

Abandoning my imaginings, I walk over to Boone, who's still pacing like a caged mountain lion.

"If you tell me what you're looking for, I can help you find it," I say.

Whatever he says is so quiet and muffled, I can't make it out.

"What was that?"

"Grave," he says. "I'm looking for a grave. Maybe more'n one."

I don't ask him why, as it seems personal enough and he seems perturbed enough already. So I simply move to another section of ground and walk back and forth like he's doing. "Is there a stone, or a cross, or something?"

"I don't know."

It's not a lot to go on, but I figure it can't be harder than searching for a nest of vampires in a series of hill caves, so I keep my eyes peeled as I traverse the dusty ground. I pass something that looks like just another rock, but the moon shadow from the bush next to it looks a little sharper than some of the other shadows. I squat down to get a better look and see there's an etching in the stone.

"Hey, Boone?" I say softly.

He's at my side in an instant, running his fingers over the engravings. They're so old, it's impossible to read them, but he must know what it says, and that's all that matters right now.

"This what you were looking for?" I ask.

When he doesn't answer, I look over at him. His face is shiny, wet.

Boone's crying.

The sight nearly knocks me on my ass. I want to scrabble away, let him have his moment alone. It's what he asked for, ain't it? I start to move. Then I remember the way he treated me when I asked for a moment, by the river. Before the fae tried to take me. How I'd tried to pull away from Boone, then eventually accepted his comfort.

And I'd felt a hundred times better.

So I don't move from my spot. I stay right where I am, the outside of my arm brushing the outside of his, and I sit tight. I don't have to do any talking, he might not welcome it. But I can bear silent witness to his pain.

"I loved this person," he says after a long while.

I nod. "It's hard to say goodbye, ain't it."

"Yeah, Boswell, it is." He reaches into his duster and

pulls out a thick book. The Bible he had earlier, looks like. He sets it down at the base of the stone.

"You want me to step away so you can have some words privately?" I ask.

He shakes his head, then runs his knuckles over his cheeks. "I'm good, Boswell. Thanks."

So we sit there together, not moving, not speaking, staring at the illegible etchings on the stone.

It can be lonesome out here in the desert prairie. But it don't have to be.

NINETEEN

WE'RE UP BEFORE DAWN, riding toward the Rift. Every piece of my body wants to revolt. But the sun begins to warm the side of my face, reminding me we have daylight on our side.

The distance is hard to gauge with all the shadows, but I reckon we have a half day until we make it to the ridge ahead, where a line in the face of the mountain curves downward like the disappointed frown of a man without his teeth. I hope it ain't too steep for Kitty; it don't sit right with me to leave her somewhere when I could be gone a couple of days.

I munch on some hardtack while we ride. Carson's chewing on jerky and smiling widely at Sheriff, who rolls her eyes. I watch Boone's back, his wide shoulders that taper to his waist. The man's all muscle.

Sheriff catches me looking. When she winks at me, I feel my cheeks color.

We reach the ridge. The horses must smell water nearby because they angle to one side of the shade, eager. Sure enough, there's a little trickle of water. I find some hardtack in one of my saddlebags and drop it into the stream while the horses drink. Damned fae. They're probably crawling all over this place. I toss in a second piece of hardtack, just to be on the safe side.

The ridge itself doesn't look too steep, and there's even a trail, likely from miners back in the day. Once Kitty's had her fill of water, I nudge her forward.

"Hold up," Sheriff says.

I turn in the saddle. "What is it?"

"Just thinking maybe we should sit a spell. Rest now, so we can be alert at night when the bloodsuckers are awake."

"I'd rather get moving," I say.

She shakes her head. "I don't agree."

"But the Browning kids—"

"They're either already dead, or they can wait a few more hours," she says.

I look at Hardin, who shrugs in about the most unhelpful way possible, his beard hiding his mouth. Carson takes a bite of jerky and says, "I agree with Sheriff."

"Boone?" I say.

He looks up quickly, like he's surprised, then his face relaxes. "Sheriff's right. It'll be better to rest now and rest easier, and then be alert at night while we're on their ground."

I close my eyes, breathe in, searching for patience. We just rested. Sure, we were up while it was still dark, but resting now just seems a mite unproductive.

"Boswell," Boone says in a quiet voice, "it's the right thing to do."

I throw up my hands. "Fine. We'll rest. But we're up and on our way before twilight."

"Sounds more'n fair," Sheriff says.

Everyone settles down in the shadow of a large boulder. I put my bedroll next to a dead tree and lean against the trunk, pulling my hat low over my forehead. Running my hand over the beads on my other wrist, I hope this hunt doesn't end in me needing to use these charms.

Sheriff and Carson fall asleep within minutes, and I envy whatever could put a heart at ease enough to let a person drift into dreamland so effortlessly. Hardin lies down, but he ain't relaxed, I can tell.

Boone remains awake, staring south, in the direction of the ruined homestead and the grave we sat next to for so long. I'll likely never know who the person was to him. Grandparent? Parent? The grave was old, I'd say maybe forty or fifty years old, maybe more. It's hard to tell, given how weather wears away stone. Whoever it was must've died when Boone was quite young, possibly before he was born. He don't look more'n ten years older than me.

Hardin has fallen asleep. He even snores—quiet enough it probably ain't a danger. Loud enough to grate on my nerves.

I move away from him, and it puts me closer to Boone. When my elbow brushes his, he doesn't jerk away, doesn't even blink at the surprise contact. I've never met a more steadfast man.

"What are you looking at out there?" I ask, gesturing to the valley.

"I ain't so sure anymore," he says.

Cryptic. Just as I open my mouth to ask for some clarification, he says, "You ever feel like the world don't want you to exist, Boswell?"

His voice is so low, I can't read the tone. I look up at his face, see him gazing down on me.

"What if *we* are the outlaws?" he asks. "We don't have a home. We deal in death."

"We don't deal with death, exactly," I say.

He grins. "Our business is in dead bodies, Gracie Boswell, you know that well as I do."

"We're protecting the humans," I say.

"But do we belong with them?" he asks.

I think on that a moment. "Maybe not. But we belong here, doing what we're doing."

"Together?" he asks.

I slide a glance back over to him like I ain't sure, but then I smile. "I suppose so."

He smiles so wide it makes my chest hurt. "I reckon I want to kiss you, Boswell."

I could probably catch flies with my open mouth, I'm so surprised. Maybe he's joking with me.

"What do you think?" he asks.

Instead of speaking, I sit up on my knees and tilt my head toward his. Those golden-brown eyes of his regard me seriously and he looks at my mouth. This kissing idea ain't a joke. Good thing, because I ain't laughing.

He presses his mouth against mine. Our breaths mingle. He tastes like a fiery sunrise consuming a valley.

His lips are embers. They ignite something inside of me. I ain't been kissed a lot and it never bothered me too much one way or another. But this. I wouldn't mind being kissed a whole lot more if the kisses are like Boone's.

Hardin snorts in his sleep, and I pull away from Boone. I can't help touching my lips. I just kissed Levi Boone.

Staring at him, I whisper, "I should...I should get some sleep, like the others. Can you keep watch?"

"Yeah, Boswell," he says, his gaze soft. "I can keep watch."

I scoot away from him, back to my bedroll against the dead tree. Leaning against it, I watch what Boone does next. I half expect him to laugh at my inexpert kissing, but he merely takes a deep breath in and out, then picks up a small rock and tosses it at Hardin.

"Hardin," Boone hisses. "Wake up and keep watch with me so Boswell can rest."

Hardin grumbles, but he opens his eyes and presses himself up into a sitting position.

I settle my hat lower on my head and stare at the darkness inside of it. I still can't believe I kissed Levi Boone, so I resolve to work that out in my dreams, maybe. It's a puzzle for later.

Eventually, I must doze, because I jerk awake to someone's arm on my shoulder.

"Boswell," Boone hisses.

I tip up my hat and look at him. He stares pointedly at Sheriff and Carson. Hardin's also looking at them, an expression of horror on his bearded face.

Sheriff and Carson are still lying on their bedrolls. They don't move, but their eyes are open and they stare at the cheerful blue sky. Their mouths are moving, lips forming the same words at the same time, but I can't hear what they're saying.

Boone grips my forearm and tugs at me. I get up and walk with him over to our sleeping companions.

The words coming from their mouths are whispers, so I lean in close. Boone hovers close by, too. Hardin doesn't move, staying a few yards off on his bedroll, which doesn't surprise me much. I make a note to never have to depend on him on my side in a fight. The man's as brave as a mouse.

"...our bounty in blood. In this land, you're the outlaws. We'll take our bounty in blood. In this land, you're the outlaws. We'll take our bounty—"

It's the same two phrases, over and over. It's what Bill said, around the time he was reciting the names of the dead.

I lean back, stunned, and focus on Boone. "What is happening?"

"Isn't it obvious?" Hardin says, eyebrows raised to make his hazel eyes bigger. "It's a message."

Boone nods.

"From the nest," I mutter. They're using the same kind of spell to transfer the message to the Sheriff's and Carson's dreams, just like they did with Bill.

The two of them are still repeating the phrases in synchrony. Their eyes flick back and forth like they're seeing something up in the sky, but when I look, there ain't nothing but a couple of clouds.

"We have to snap them out of it," I say. "Whatever's making them do this can't be good."

"I agree." Boone reaches for Carson's arm and shakes him.

I grab the Sheriff's arm and tug. Neither she nor Carson wakes.

"Come on, Sheriff, wake up," I say. "This is just a bad dream."

Sheriff goes rigid on her bedroll, legs and arms straight out. Then she screams. I want to leap away and cover my ears, but whatever she's seeing, it ain't good, and I can't leave her in a dream like that. I shake her shoulders and yell over her scream. "Sheriff! Wake up!"

She's still screaming, long and drawn-out, unending. I do the only thing I can think to do, and I slap her.

The pain must jerk her awake because she stops screaming and sits up, then scrambles back out of my reach, a panicked expression on her face. Carson's doing the same, struggling to get away from Boone. Lifting his hands, Boone lets Carson go.

Carson and Sheriff remain sitting, both of 'em panting like they just raced across the desert. Carson rubs a hand over his face, back and forth, like he's trying to scrub something off of him. Sheriff looks frozen to her spot.

"Are you all right?" I ask, looking from one to the other. If they go quiet like Bill was, I don't know what we'll do with them, this far away from Penance. Could Hardin manage to take them both back to town?

"It was horrible," Carson says in a harsh whisper, much like the one he was using to relay the message.

Sheriff nods.

My pa always encouraged me to talk about my bad

dreams, but I'm afraid to hear about what Carson and Sheriff endured. Besides, they ain't kids. Still, I make the offer. "Would it help to describe it?"

Sheriff shakes her head. "I don't want to relive it. I just want to forget."

"Are you aware you were speaking while you were asleep?" Boone asks.

"No," Carson and Sheriff say at once.

"What was I saying?" Carson asks.

"It was the same for both of you," I say. "The same as Bill said, too. 'We'll take our bounty in blood. In this land, you're the outlaws.'"

They're quiet a moment. We're all likely thinking of what it could mean, why the vampires are sending the message.

"It ain't the words that were scary," Sheriff says. "It was the images."

Carson nods. "Outlaws fighting humans. Outlaws fighting each other. Blood everywhere, coating the buildings, painting the prairie. Is that what you saw, Sheriff?"

"Yes. Vampires were fighting fae, demons. Shapeshifters were tearing people apart. Fae were grabbing humans and outlaws alike, dragging them into rivers."

"Vampires fighting fae?" Hardin says. "I wonder who'd win. I'd put my gold on—"

"Shut up, Hardin," Sheriff says in a tired voice. "What do you think of this, Gracie?"

"I think it's good," I say.

Sheriff and Carson look at me like I've gone mad.

"It means we're close," I say. "They're trying to intimidate us, make us feel as if our efforts will be fruitless. But we're close, and they're scared of us. That's what it means."

Nobody says anything. I wonder if that means they agree, or disagree, but I don't much care one way or the other. My gut's telling me that I'm right.

"I'm done with resting," Carson says. "I say we ride."

I look at Sheriff. She was the one who'd insisted on stopping. The sun's still fairly high.

"I say we ride, too," Sheriff says, scooting toward me and gripping my wrist so hard, the healing charms dig into my flesh and bruise my bones. "We have to keep them from winning. I can't bear to see that dream come to pass. I can't bear to see Penance drenched in blood."

TWENTY

THE TRAIL IS dusty and overgrown, and the nearby hill isn't high enough to protect us from the sun, which bakes my braid against my back. We pick our way among the rubble and the sparse vegetation that creeps into our path like bony arms.

Our horses plod along, ears flicking this way and that. They likely sense our tension and it has them as nervous as we are.

Hardin starts talking. "Whiskey," he says. "What I wouldn't give for a whiskey and a nice game of cards with some gullible cowherds."

"Hush," I say.

To his credit, he listens.

Until he points at the ground and shouts, "Rattler," so loud, it spooks his own horse. He recovers control quickly, but I'm losing my temper.

"Do you want everyone in the territory to hear you?" I snap.

"Apologies," he says. His face is sweaty, his eyes round with fear.

We shouldn't have brought a barkeep along. I send an aggrieved glance to the sheriff, who shrugs her shoulders.

I'm tired of being too hot, of being too thirsty, of being surrounded by other souls. Sheriff, Boone, and Carson ain't too bad, but I'll be right glad to be rid of Hardin when this is over.

Just as we cross a patch of brush, a hit from nowhere knocks me clean from my saddle. I don't even see it. One minute I'm comfortable enough on my horse, and the next I'm flat on my back, a brittlebush digging into my ass. Kitty's side-stepping away and looks ready to bolt.

I rub my head, disoriented, and look for everyone else. Boone's the only one of us still mounted on his horse. A shadowy form embraces him from the back, light bending around it in the strange way it bends around Boone sometimes, like my eyes ain't seeing it clearly. Boone reaches back and grabs the creature by the neck and lifts it off him. He tosses the form to the side and looks around quickly until his gaze lands on me.

I stare at him in shock. Him picking the creature off him that way shouldn't be possible. No man can just grab another like that and fling him away like he's a garter snake.

Not only that, the creature he tossed aside is a vampire.

It's daylight. This isn't possible. Their skin should be burning, peeling from their bones in the sun.

"Behind you, Boswell," he says.

No time to think, I spin around and haul myself to my knees, stake outstretched in one move. The vampire either doesn't see the stake or doesn't care, because it runs right at me. Bracing myself for the impact, I hold the stake steady and thrust as the vampire gets close. There's a sick, wet, crunching sound as the stake goes into its chest.

I leave the stake where it is and kick the vampire over. I'll behead it later. Two vampires are on Carson, one with its mouth on his neck. I lift my pistol, and as soon as I'm confident in my aim, I let loose a charm.

The vampire goes down, stunned for now, but I know the charm won't last long. My building headache will be lasting much longer. Gripping another stake, I lunge forward.

Carson's wrestling with the second vampire. Boone's struggling with another one but has the upper hand. Sheriff and Hardin are nowhere in sight, and their horses are careening down the trail. I hope the horses don't go too far, but now ain't the time to calm their panic and recover them. I run to Carson and jab his opponent with my stake. The vampire pivots at the last second and I miss. My momentum throws me forward and I stumble into Carson, thankfully missing him with the stake. He grabs my elbows to steady me, then whips me behind him as another vampire advances.

Confusion fills me even as I look to the next vampire to fight. The bloodsuckers shouldn't be out, not without their skin burning. Yet these ones are gleefully waging a battle with us.

And more are coming down the hillside.

It's all whirling chaos. I shoot several charms from my

pistol, as do Carson and Boone. I don't know where the hell the sheriff and Hardin went off to, but we could really use their help about now.

I fire off charms at a vampire coming straight at me, knock it down. I look at my pistol and fumble with extra charms in my pocket so I can re-load. One charm goes in, and another. My head already aches from the spent charms. My hands are shaking with my fear and need to be quick, and I glance up to make sure no vampires are too close.

Arms grip me from behind. They lock around my elbows, pulling back my shoulders, squeezing. I can't hang onto my pistol, and it clatters to the dust.

"You're mine, charmslinger," a rough voice says in my ear.

Boone and Carson are busy with their own opponents. I yank against the hold on my arms, but I can't pull away. Cool lips press against my neck. A feeling of revulsion overwhelms me.

"No," I whisper.

"Yes," the vampire croons in a woman's voice. I turn and see a braid draping down next to a sweet face. It's Sarah Alice, one of the vampires from the wanted poster.

I try to stomp on its foot, but I can't see where it's standing and my heels hit the ground. Pulling at my arms only brings pain. I pull anyway. I'd rather pop out my shoulder than be killed by a bloodsucker.

Sharp pain, and a burning in my neck as Sarah Alice's teeth sink in. Some victims go limp, I've seen, subdued by whatever poison the vampire carries. Not all, though. Some struggle more.

I'm in the latter category. I flail with my legs, kicking everything I can reach. My stakes are right there—right there, strapped to my leg, but I don't have use of my arms.

Nothing I do has any effect on the vampire, and its mouth is cool against my neck. I can feel the pull of blood leaving my body.

I can do this—I've fought worse. I've had one foot in the grave. A bite don't mean I'll be a vampire, just like Carson won't be. Not unless I die here.

And I don't aim to die here.

Bending forward, I try to lift Sarah Alice. But I don't have Boone's strength. The teeth in my neck only tear more flesh as I move. If it tears an artery, I truly will die. I go still, and the vampire makes a soft crooning noise against my neck, like it's trying to soothe me.

I ain't soothed.

Carson's kneeling on the chest of his opponent, stake held high. Boone's throwing one off his back while another one advances, ready to take its place. I catch a glimpse of dusty gray fabric half-hidden behind a rock, and a black leather boot—that would be Hardin. His leg is motionless.

It ain't looking good. No one's going to rescue me, which, until I met Boone and Carson, was pretty much the story of my life. How quickly I went soft, I think, hoping for rescue. Having a posse has spoiled me, made me dependent on others.

Maybe I will die here. I hope Carson or Boone stakes me or takes off my head before I have a chance to rise. I don't want to be a bloodsucker, I'll walk into the sun first. Least, that's what I tell myself now. I wonder how many people have died at the hands of bloodsuckers with the intent of walking into the sun, only to be changed when they rise. Pa was out of his right mind. He never would've harmed me otherwise.

The air's suddenly cool against my neck, breeze hitting the blood. Sarah Alice lets me go, whirls away in braids and blood. My arms are freed. I don't even wait for the feeling to come back to them all the way. I flop my left hand down, even though it's numb, and reach for a stake. It takes me a bit longer than usual to grip one, but when I finally do, I hold it up, ready to throw or stab.

But there's nothing here. Nobody but Boone, Carson, and me.

"Where'd they go?" I say, spinning around to look at the trail, at the rocks below and above us.

There's no sign of the deader than dead vampires, either. Did the others take the bodies with them? Maybe they're hoping they'll rise again.

Carson's pressing a handkerchief to his bleeding neck. Boone's inspecting a tear on his shirt, but I don't see any blood beneath it. Hardin's leg is still unmoving. My head pounds something fierce, but I'm alive.

As there's no immediate danger—and I still can't figure out why, or even why there was danger to begin with—I move to Hardin.

His chest is rising and falling, so I kneel next to him and shake his shoulder. "Hardin. Hardin, are you all right?"

He mumbles something incoherent and his eyes flutter open. "What happened? I was knocked out, missed the whole thing."

"We were ambushed. Broad daylight." I turn to the others. "Find the sheriff, I haven't seen her."

Hardin gestures to a ways down the trail. "She took off, I think."

"She wouldn't do that," I say.

Sitting up, Hardin frowns at me. "Just how well do you know Sheriff, Miss Boswell?"

I shake my head. I don't know her well, but I know she wouldn't run during a fight. Even Hardin stuck around. Injured and useless, sure, but he was here. Sheriff wouldn't leave. "I'm gonna look for her."

"I'll help." Hardin tries to stand, but falls back.

My heart squeezes with sympathy—he looks pitiful and frustrated.

"Wait here a spell," I say, touching his shoulder gently. He doesn't even flinch, which is progress for our very tentative camaraderie. "Get your balance again."

Instead of tearing down the trail to look for the sheriff, I go up a ways. Boone and Carson join me while Hardin sits against a rock, recovering.

"Sheriff!" I call, then wince as the volume of my voice exacerbates my headache. "Sheriff!"

Boone's next to me, looking on one side of the trail while I look on the other. Carson takes the trail back in the direction Hardin points, although I'm sure he, like me, doesn't truly believe she retreated. But maybe she was dragged?

The brush and boulders aren't giving up their secrets easily. I half expect to find a nest of vampires taking shelter in the shade, but there's nothing. No sign of struggle. Footprints dot the trail, though I can't tell whether any of them might be Sheriff's.

Carson runs up. "She ain't at the lower end of the trail, so I'll help you two up here."

While we search, I say to them, "How did this happen? Why didn't they burn in the daylight?"

"Yeah, Boone, how is that possible?" Carson asks in a strange voice.

"They could've been using some kind of charm," Boone says. "There's a light-bending charm. It must've been weak, inexpensive, and doesn't last long, is my guess."

"I found her," Carson says, his voice urgent.

I rush up the trail to his side. He's turning Sheriff over from where she'd been lying face down in the brush.

TWENTY-ONE

"NO," I gasp, kneeling next to Sheriff.

A large gash rips across her torso from her chest to her hip. There's a lot of blood. It stains the checked cloth of her blouse, soaking into the fabric, smearing the dirt and stone beneath her.

So much blood. It seems more'n a body should be able to hold. Maybe someone else got hurt here, and some of this is theirs.

I know I'm grasping at wild, impossible hope. I can't help it, though.

Boone comes up to us and kneels at Sheriff's head. He touches her neck, his face grave. "She's dead."

Dead. My mind tumbles over that ugly word, and it thuds loud in my heart, causing it to thump with a need for action. I have to move. There's something I can do, something that I, as a charmslinger, know how to do. Because she can't be dead.

Already I'm ripping a strand of beads from my wrist.

I slide it into her palm. It needs some blood, which between the two of us we have plenty of. Then I'll speak a word. And it'll save her.

Boone stops my hand when I reach for my bleeding neck. "It won't work," he says. "She's gone."

"This charm'll bring someone back from the edge of the grave," I say.

"She's not standing on the edge looking in," Boone says softly. "She's dead. And there ain't no magic short of necromancy or vampirism can bring a body back from the dead, Boswell."

"Whoa-whoa-whoa," Carson says. "No necromancy. Sheriff wouldn't want that."

"It ain't necromancy!" I shout. "It'll heal her."

Ignoring Boone's sound of dismay, I run my fingertips over the wound in my neck, then over the beads in Sheriff's hand.

I murmur, "Heal."

Then I wait.

The beads flash with blue light before returning to their original black and gray. Sheriff's chest ain't moving, and while some of her broken skin knits together, it falls right back apart again.

Ignoring the sign that my efforts are in vain, and I take off my second healing charm.

"No, Boswell," Boone says. "It ain't going to save her. Look at her, she's already gone. Let her go."

"I can't accept that." I shove the beads into her palm next to the others. Her skin is clammy and cool. I can't do this, I can't let her die.

This time it's Carson who says, "Gracie, don't waste that charm on a dead woman."

"She *ain't dead*," I say, even though a part of me knows she is. I swipe blood from my neck to the beads. I close my eyes and whisper, "Heal."

Opening my eyes, I see the beads flash with a blue haze. Sheriff's body flinches as her wound knits together at one end. It splits apart again immediately like it did the first time, and I curse.

"Come on," I say. "Sheriff, come back to us."

Boone looks on, face stoic, light brown eyes full of regret. He shakes his head.

"She ain't breathing," Carson says in a soft voice, as if I'm a scared horse he's afraid of spooking. "Let her go, Gracie."

"No." I take off the last bracelet, the one I purchased in Shepherd before this whole foolish escapade began.

Boone's hand is warm on my wrist as he holds me back. "Gracie. She's gone. Don't waste your charms."

"It's not a waste if I can save her."

"You can't save her," Boone says from behind me. He pulls me against him. Voice quiet, he says, "She's really and truly gone. I'm sorry."

I try to see Sheriff's chest, to see if it's lifting up and down, but my vision's all blurry. I clutch my sight charm, thinking it must be faulty. It's the tears in my eyes, though. I dash them away with my knuckles and struggle against Boone's hold. "It's worth a chance."

"There's no chance, Gracie." Carson looks as devastated as I am.

I can't fight Boone's grasp anymore; my body's too

exhausted. I go limp against him, spouting curses that would make my pa's face turn red if he were alive to hear them. Boone's restriction turns into an embrace. I feel the pain in his arms, in the tight way he holds himself.

"She can't be gone," I say.

"She is," Boone says quietly. "I'm so sorry. I'm so damned sorry."

He holds me while our breathing returns to normal. Carson stands awkwardly nearby, a sorrowful expression on his face. Finally, I pull away from Boone.

Sheriff's eyes are open, staring blankly at the sky. The coils of beads in her hand are dull, smeared with my blood, all magic gone.

"I wish you hadn't wasted those," Carson says, following my gaze.

I don't have room for that kind of regret. It doesn't feel like a waste to me—not before, not now. I thought she had a chance, and I had to give it to her. I'd never be able to live with myself otherwise. So no, I can't be angry at myself.

But I can be angry at the bloodsuckers who took her life. Even thinking of how we were attacked like this, in broad daylight, thinking of how they want to use us, hold us down, keep humans like cattle, gets my blood boiling.

"I hate them," I say. The words feel so true, so dark and powerful in my mouth, that I say it again. "I *hate* them."

Boone jerks, like someone hit him with a cattle brand.

I say it a third time as my heart pumps fast and hard, a dark haze coming over my vision. "I hate them."

"I do, too," Carson says. His eyes are shining, like he's

got tears he hasn't let fall yet. His face is pale, hands bloody. Whose blood, I can't say. Could be his own, or mine, or Sheriff's.

Too much blood has been spilled because of vampires. They're ruining this land.

Standing up, I face the rocky side of the mountain, examining every little crevice and hollow, wondering where those cowards are hiding now.

"Rift take you!" I shout at the mountains, the shadows, the whole godforsaken landscape. They're hiding somewhere in these parts, and I know they can hear me, wherever they are.

My throat's raw, burning from the rage I send through it. This isn't fair. It doesn't make sense to me that good people have to die when others live. Sheriff was worth twelve of me. She was a good person, a good sheriff, a brave soul. And now she's gone.

Carson's voice is low, but it's filled with the same fury I feel. "I don't know why you're looking for them up there to shout at 'em."

I turn slowly, taking in his angry gaze. His brows are drawn together, his fists clenched. He ain't looking at me, though—he's looking directly at Boone.

"What are you talking about?" I ask.

"Pup," Boone says, his low voice a warning.

Carson laughs, but it's the kind of laugh that's lost all its sugar. Bitter as water left in an old canteen in the sun. He says, "You don't need to shout up yonder to curse a vampire, Gracie. You've got one right in front of you."

Boone growls. "Damn you, pup."

I'm ready to throw something, but what, I don't know.

I want to attack, I want to tear something apart. Taking a deep breath to keep from screaming, I say, "I'll ask you one more time, Carson. *What are you talking about?*"

"There's a bloodsucker. Right there." Carson lifts his arm and slowly points at Boone.

TWENTY-TWO

IT SHOULD BE funny how slow it happens. Impossibly slow. First I take in the darkening sky. The sun's going down, just the remains of it coming over a nearby hill, hitting the top half of this mountain. It even hits Boone, who's standing, his golden-brown eyes hard and clear as he faces me and Carson.

The light weaves around him, same way as it did the first time I saw him in the daytime, that morning at Hardin's saloon.

I see the charm on his wrist, the intricate network of beads and leather. I guessed it had taken a witch days to create, that it was expensive as anything they had to offer, that it would save a body from the grave several times over.

It ain't a healing charm, though, like I'd first assumed. It's a light-bending charm, and it's saving Boone from the sunlight, day in, day out.

And Boone needs it because he is a vampire.

Boone's brown eyes grow dark with anger. He forms a

fist. He pulls back his arm. His intention is clear. Carson has plenty of time to dodge, but he stays put next to me. Boone's clenched fist makes contact with Carson's jaw.

Carson flies back, lands on his ass in the dirt, rubs his chin and cheek.

"I deserved that," Carson says.

"Reckon you did," Boone says.

They both look at me.

I say nothing at first. A breeze rushes through the dead tree branches, moves Boone's duster around his legs. He's a vampire. This bounty hunter who's scooped out bounties from underneath me the past few years, this man who saved my life at least once and possibly more, this person I've come to think of as a friend—is a vampire.

"Did you have anything to do with the attack just now?" I ask him.

"No. The vampires killed my kin. Now I kill them."

I don't know why I should believe him. He's a vampire. But his motivation aligns with mine. And my deep-seated hatred conflicts with what I thought I knew —I thought I knew Boone was a good man. I thought he was a human, a bounty hunter, and a charmslinger like me.

Now I know he's an outlaw.

Is he still the same person, though? I can't work it out.

My brain can't settle. Boone's completely still, a statue of himself, and his face is carefully blank. Does he think I'm going to send him away? I don't know what's best.

Then I look down at Sheriff's body, her eyes unblinking. I reach for my knife, hand it to Carson. "Take off her head. I'll go down and find the horses."

I know Carson doesn't like blood or the gorier parts of this work. But he takes the knife and nods.

Neither Boone nor Carson speak as I walk away. I pass Hardin on the side of the trail. He's sitting with his knees pulled up, folded arms atop them, head resting there. He doesn't look up when I approach, which suits me fine. I can't bear to tell him about Sheriff.

Life is full of things I think I can't bear, so I go ahead and say it. "Sheriff's dead."

He looks up, his hazel eyes pained. "She—she is?"

I can't say it again, so I nod. "We're going to bury her. Then...then I don't know."

I move past him to retrieve the horses. Luckily for me, they haven't gone far, not even to the bottom of the hill. I reach for Kitty, stroke her neck. I click my tongue and all five horses follow me back up the trail.

The sun's falling fast and it's twilight when the horses and I make it back to the others. The vampires'll come out again soon. Sheriff's getting a shallow grave, which pains me, but I don't reckon we have a choice.

Seeing Sheriff's decapitated body is not the worst thing I've ever had to view in my life, but it's surely among the worst. I understood, at the time, why she didn't want to remove the head of the Browning son, but the feeling hits harder when it's her neck that Carson's sawing on.

I pull the short spade from Kitty's saddlebag and get to work on a grave at the side of the trail. It ain't a bad place for a final rest, I suppose, with a view of this pretty valley, dotted with grasses and flowering bushes.

Boone silently gets another spade and digs as well. A couple of times he inhales quickly like he's about to speak, but no words come.

I have nothing to say to him, and I don't much care to listen at the moment, neither. I know he's not a bad guy—at least, I don't think he is.

Letting my thoughts swirl like a tornado in my mind, I pull spadefuls of dirt from the earth.

The grave isn't big, but it's going to be full dark soon, so it'll have to do. Carson and I drag over Sheriff's body, and Boone carries the head. Hardin sits on a rock, hat in his hands. We lower Sheriff into the grave and I say, "I didn't know her well, but I liked her. She was kind. She was funny. She cared about her son."

I picture that young man, Wesley, and I already regret that I'll have to tell him his ma is dead.

"I liked her too," Carson says.

Boone doesn't speak, but he grips the brim of his hat hard while he holds it against his chest.

We don't have time for more speeches or farewells. Boone and I pile the dirt back on top of Sheriff, filling the hole, covering her torn body and head, hiding her beauty and bravery from the rest of the world forever. Carson rolls a big stone over and sets it atop the grave.

The sun is fully down now. The vampires could come out again, any minute.

I wish there was more to say for Sheriff. I wish we'd had more time—not just now, for goodbyes, but in life, to get to know her better.

"We need to ride," I say, patting my sheath and holster. My pistol's missing. "Where's my gun?"

"A vampire made you drop it during the fight, just over there," Hardin says, swinging up onto his horse.

I'd forgotten that. "Thanks."

As I walk a few yards back on the trail to retrieve my weapon, a chill spreads through me. All Hardin's loud noises, scuffing sounds. And now this.

"Wait just a moment," I say, turning back around to face him.

Something flashes in his eyes—alarm—then it's gone just as fast.

He's disguising his emotions. Maybe not well, but he's trying.

"You said you were knocked out, that you missed the fight," I say. "You asked me what happened."

"Yes, that's right."

"So how'd you know how and where I dropped my pistol?"

The alarm flashes across his face again. "Well, I must have guessed about your pistol—"

"He's lyin'," Carson says.

Hardin grabs his own pistol and raises it on me. I've got nothing—my gun's still in the dirt at my feet. Carson reaches for his holster, but Hardin says, "Don't touch your weapon or I'll shoot her. Put your hands on your head. All of you—even you, vampire."

Hardin and Boone raise their hands. From the corner of my eye I can see their faces. Tense, furious.

"I don't understand," I say to Hardin, lifting my hands up. I don't know what kind of nasty thing he has in his pistol, but given his disdain for charmslingers, and how he killed that fae, I'm going to guess it's a real bullet. "You're helping the vampires?"

"I'm surprised it took you this long to figure it out," he says. "Even a barkeep knows how to walk quiet in the hills, but I never managed to."

"And you killed the new vampire before it could lead us to the others," I say.

He nods. "Now you're catching on."

I remember something else. "Your wife said you were sleeping in that morning in Penance. But later, when we found the red fabric from the Browning girl's dress—you said that was what she wore when she rode out. You shouldn't have known what she was wearing if you were sleeping."

"Exactly. I wasn't sleepin'," he says. "I saw the Brownings ride out just as I finished starting the church on fire."

"Why?" I ask.

"The vampires told me to."

He says his piece without remorse, without emotion. I'd thought him a bumbling fool, but he's a lying, two-faced piece of excrement.

"But why would you help them?" I ask.

"Simple. I help them, they don't harm me or my family."

"You save your family at the cost of the entire town—your neighbors and friends," I say, disgusted.

He shrugs. "I was taught to protect my own above all others. And letting you live, now, goes against my own."

His finger tightens on the trigger; I can see from the way his forearm flexes that he's getting ready to shoot me.

For the second time today, I think I'm going to die.

A bang. A flash of light. I brace myself for the pain, but nothing touches me. Instead, Hardin falls off his saddle. His horse rears and flees.

I jump, startled, immediately looking to Carson. His hands are still on his head. It's Boone who holds the smoking pistol. It ain't his charm pistol, either.

I don't waste any time; I grab the pistol at my feet and run to Hardin. He hasn't moved, and he doesn't move except for when I turn him over with my boot. A bullet entered his forehead.

"He's dead," I say to Carson, then flick my glance to Boone. "Why'd you kill him?"

"He was going to shoot you," Boone says.

"Just that reason alone?" I ask. "You weren't afraid he'd implicate you, a vampire, in any of this?"

As soon as the accusation is out of my mouth, I want to take it back.

"Apologies, that ain't fair," I say, holstering my gun.

"Maybe not, but it's how you really feel," Boone says. He tips his hat. His eyes are difficult to make out in the darkness, but I think I read pain there.

"It's not—"

"I can see I've lost your trust," Boone says. "I'll go."

I should tell him not to. I should ask him to stay, tell him we need his help. But I can't make my lips form the words. And then he and Pegasus are riding off, not up the trail or down it, but sideways through the rocks and scrub brush.

It takes me a minute to realize what just happened. Boone's leaving. No, he left.

I look at Carson. Carson looks at me. He rubs a hand over his face.

Sheriff's dead. Hardin's dead—which is more of an advantage than him being alive, I suppose. Boone's gone.

"I'm done," I say to Carson.

He gapes. "What?"

"Done. It's over."

"What about Penance?" he asks.

"What about it? It's a Rift town, and every soul in there will pack up and move away if they know what's good for them. I'll ride through and give them a warning before traveling south."

Carson shakes his head. He disagrees, but he's not arguing. I wonder what words he's holding back.

I kick Hardin's boot. Sheriff got a grave, and a poor one at that. I'm not about to do even that much for a coward and a betrayer.

"Food for the buzzards," Carson says.

"That's my thought, too."

After giving Hardin one last scathing glance, I whirl around and climb into Kitty's saddle.

"Wait, where are you going?" Carson asks.

"Away," I say.

Carson keeps at me. "What's our plan?"

"We don't have a plan. You're going to go off and do whatever you want, and I'm going to go off and do whatever I want. The hunt's over, the posse's disbanded, and I reckon that's the end of it."

He stares. "So that's it? You're just going to leave like that?"

"Yep."

"I'm coming with you," he says.

"I don't want a shadow, pup." Boone's nickname for Carson slides off my tongue without me giving it a second thought.

I click my tongue to get Kitty walking.

"I didn't take you for mean," Carson says from behind me.

"Then you never knew me." I keep riding, sad and satisfied when he doesn't get on his horse and follow. I didn't mean to be mean, but the effect is the same, and the empty place in my chest is too full of darkness to have any room for regrets.

Kitty's as eager to get off this mountain as I am, and we move down the trail immediately, Sheriff's and Hardin's horses trailing behind, Carson and his horse left in our dust.

I urge Kitty to go faster. I don't want to look back at Carson, I don't want to think about Sheriff, or Boone. All I want is to get away. Give the horses back to Penance. Tell them about the nest's plans. Find a quiet piece of land somewhere far, far south of the Rift.

TWENTY-THREE

AS WE TRAVEL DOWN the trail, I half expect the nest to ambush us again. It's what I'd do. So I encourage Kitty to go faster.

I used to think I was the kind of charmslinger who'd rather die than let the vampires triumph.

I used to think I was the kind of charmslinger who stood up for what was right.

I used to think I was the kind of charmslinger who used the magic, who saved the town, who protected those who couldn't protect themselves.

Turns out, I'm none of those things. I'm the kind of charmslinger who slinks off into the night, licking her wounds and hiding from the outlaws. My neck twinges where the vampire bit it. A new scar to go along with the one Pa gave me. I could use a mending stone, but I don't want to. I'd rather feel the pain of this. The bleeding's stopped, which is good enough for now.

I'm taking the most direct route to Penance, roughly east from the mining mountains and the Rift we'd been approaching. It pulls me through the shadows of hills, but I'm no longer afraid of what's in here. Let an outlaw take me. Let it be over.

It isn't until we're far into the valley, nearly an hour into our ride, that pounding hooves pull my focus from the moon-washed landscape in front of me.

"Gracie," Carson calls. "Gracie!"

I turn in my saddle. He's close behind, and his voice is frantic but his stance is just as handsome and majestic as always. The gorgeous cowherd, who I thought was too cowardly and pretty to join our little posse. Yet he's the one here with me at the end.

He pulls his horse up alongside Kitty. The other two horses keep going in the direction of Penance. Probably for the best. I'll arrive either with the horses or soon after to give Wesley and Mrs. Hardin the news of Sheriff's and Hardin's deaths. The horses' arrival should tell them all they need to know, though, and my heart feels sorry at the thought.

It ain't fair. None of this is fair.

But nothing ever was, and the unfairness only got bigger when the Rift opened.

Carson's eyes are blue even in the moonlight and he stares intently at my face. "Gracie, I wanted to apologize. I shouldn't have said anything about Boone."

"How long did you know?" I ask, although I'm not sure it matters.

"Since the first night I joined you. When he tackled me off my horse."

I think back to that night, at the tension between

them. The constant needling, the dislike. "And you didn't see fit to tell me?"

He shakes his head. "I knew he was still an asset to the hunt. He ain't a traitor, not like Hardin."

"It doesn't matter much, anyhow," I say, then continue riding toward Penance.

"Gracie, don't ignore me," he says.

I urge Kitty to go faster and she does, but Carson's galloping along, trying to catch up. He pulls alongside me, a little in front, and slows down. Kitty has to slow, too, so as not to ram into him and his horse.

"What do you want, Carson?" I say.

"I want you to stop." His voice is low, rough with emotion. "I want you to go back up that mountain with me."

"I can't. I give up. It's over."

"It ain't over," he says.

I turn Kitty around him and continue, although not as fast.

"Gracie, this ain't like you," Carson says.

"Already told you. You don't know me. You know nothing about me."

"I know you're kind. You're brave—"

I hold up a hand. "Enough."

"No," he says, louder. "It ain't enough until you come back with me and we finish that nest off."

"Finish?" I laugh. "We ain't even started on it, Carson. We're outnumbered. Outmatched."

"No we're not. Boone's up there right now."

"Boone left, too."

"He didn't."

I shake my head, close my eyes. "He did, I saw him do it, and he had every right to."

"He didn't, he's up on that mountain right now, searching for the nest."

My path is clear, I chose it on the mountain. I'm done with this hunt and all the humans and outlaws involved in it. "Get out of my way, Carson. This is over."

He pulls his horse up. "No. We're going back for Boone."

"Don't make me hex you, pup," I say, reaching for my pistol.

Sitting taller in his saddle, he shakes his head. "You're better than that, Gracie. Come on."

My eyes sting. Blinking hard, I rub my eyes with my knuckles and growl. "No, I'm not better than that. This is who I am, Carson. Everyone wants to see the charm-slinger as something or someone different, but in the end, I'm just me, all right? I'm not a hero, I'm not brave. I'm motivated by gold and hatred, and the gold and hatred in this hunt ain't enough to keep me going. So that's the end of it."

"I don't believe you. Boone's up there, Gracie. Fighting on his own. That grave you sat at with him? I think that was his wife. He's fighting to make sure this doesn't happen to other homesteads."

His wife. I'd thought the grave belonged to someone much older. I'd thought he was a kid when they died, because I didn't know he was ageless, a vampire.

Kitty paws the ground, her ears up and alert while I process everything Carson said.

"I ain't a good, brave person," I say.

"I disagree, but I can't convince you otherwise, I suppose," Carson says.

I nod.

Encouraged by my nod, Carson goes on, "He'll be deader than dead if we don't help him. Vampire or not, he can't go up against this nest by himself."

"I reckon you're right," I say, tugging Kitty's reins to bring her around.

Carter grins, a blindingly handsome smile that shines even in the shadows of the night. Eyes on mine, he says, "Let's ride?"

"Let's ride."

We race back to the mountain. I'm extra glad for Kitty's sight charm woven into her bridle, and I hope Carson has something similar for his horse. I suspect he does, because the horse gallops forward without any hint of trepidation.

Shadows of the moon through the trees and clouds dapple the path. The air holds a chill and an urgency I haven't felt before. I've been such a fool.

I've faced more than one dismissive or outright rude act from other humans, just because I'm a charmslinger. There was the group of cowherds who tried to corner me behind that saloon in Baptism, thinking that because I was a charmslinger I was less of a person and they could take what they wanted from me. There's the marshals and sheriffs who think they don't have to give me bounties after I complete a hunt. There's the barkeeps who don't want to serve me, the ranchers who won't give me quarter when I'm traveling, the children who shout insults at me that they should be too young to know.

I've never liked being judged because of what I look like or the kind of job I have. And although I can't control my sex or my appearance, I *can* control my job.

Boone can't control whether or not he's a vampire. Yet I'm judging him for that.

I have to fix this.

We don't pause at the base of the mountain, although the horses have to go a little slower on the narrow trail. We move faster than we did during the day, with only two of us, and with knowing we can't let Boone die. Passing Sheriff's grave gives me both a pang of sorry and a renewed sense of desperation.

People die out here. Killed by the elements, by the creatures, and by the outlaws.

I can't see Boone killed next.

We keep going, fast as the horses can go. A small stream of water crosses the trail ahead of us. Carson starts to slow his horse, probably to find a piece of hardtack to throw in the water.

"No time," I say. "Keep going."

He doesn't question me, just urges his horse forward. We can worry about the stream on our way back—if we make it back.

A little ways farther, and Carson holds up a hand and I urge Kitty to halt. I cock my head, listening. Faint sounds of a struggle reach my ears, coming from over the rise of the trail. Pointing to it, I look at Carson. He nods.

We dismount and loop the horses' reins over some scrub brush. As we hurry on foot over the trail, I spy Pegasus standing ahead, shifting from foot to foot in fear. She doesn't bolt, the brave thing.

There ahead of us is the entrance to the mine. It's a black mouth in the side of a craggy mountain face.

And within it are monsters.

I look to Carson and nod. His face is grim, but determined.

Inside the mine, my sight charm has to work extra hard. If it weren't for the charm, I wouldn't be able to see my own hand in front of me. As it is, I can hold my pistol up and know that I'll be able to tell who I'm shooting when it comes time to shoot.

A thud of flesh hitting flesh and a grunt of pain draw my attention to the far left.

There, Boone's on his back, one vampire holding down his legs. A second vampire, Beatrice, is sitting on Boone's torso, a wicked knife in hand.

Beatrice lifts the knife.

I'll never reach them in time.

TWENTY-FOUR

BOONE'S GOING TO DIE, right here in front of my eyes.

And he's going to die at the hands of a vampire *I* freed.

My gun's out of my holster, warm in my hand, and I pull the trigger as Beatrice stabs.

The charm doesn't hit Beatrice in time—the knife makes contact with Boone's throat, the charm hits a second later. My gut tightens with dismay.

"He'll live, he's a vampire," Carson says, tugging me forward. "On your right."

I look where he's pointing, and three more vampires are approaching. "Take care of Boone," I shout.

Carson joins me. "He's already up."

I spare a glance over my shoulder, and sure enough, Boone's throwing off Beatrice's stunned form and he's already staking the vampire that had been sitting on his knees. Before I can turn away again, Boone looks up and his gaze connects with mine. The chaos surrounding us seems to slow, as does my heartbeat and my breathing.

An understanding flashes in his eyes, a connection. There's also trepidation there. He's worried about what I think. *I'm here for you. I respect you*, I try to tell him, before whirling around to embed my stake into one of the vampires approaching me.

Unspoken, like the rest of my thoughts: *I'm sorry I doubted you.*

The fighting is almost too fast to track. I don't have the speed or skills to pay attention to the battles going on with Boone and Carson; I can only watch the vampires that approach me. The next one to come forward is faster than I'm used to. Its long braids whip behind it as it moves—it's Sarah Alice. It grabs my wrist that holds a stake and squeezes. The strength in the grip takes my breath away. My bones ache. If the vampire grabs me any harder, I reckon they'll crack.

"Let go," Sarah Alice says, its face close to mine. Fangs dip below its upper lip. Its breath is cold and smells of blood, of decayed flowers. It smells like a grave.

I drop the stake, which clatters to the hard-packed dirt and stone floor.

Sarah Alice squeezes my arm harder and leans forward to lick the dried blood on my neck. I grit my teeth. I won't give the outlaw the satisfaction of hearing me whimper. Instead, I pull against its grip while I kick out toward it, distracting it from my real goal—my pistol.

Sarah Alice has been so intent on the stake in my one hand, it's missed the danger I hold in my other. I'm afraid to lift the gun lest the vampire see it, so I hope I'm aiming true and keep it pointed slightly down. Then I pull the trigger.

The light of the charm is the briefest of flashes, blinding me momentarily in the darkness, and then it hits its target—the vampire's leg.

Sarah Alice drops.

Quickly, I stake the heart, jabbing hard and feeling the point of the stake touch the ground beneath it.

Head aching, I look around for whatever bloodsucker is approaching next. Carson's grappling with one vampire, and Boone with another. Carson's closer and looks like he might lose his fight, his body held in the vampire's cruel embrace, so I take aim with my pistol and fire, hoping Carson won't get in the way of the charm.

He doesn't, and that vampire drops, too. Carson quickly stakes it.

The two of us face three more bloodsuckers who are eager to tussle. Side by side, Carson and I stun them with our pistols and stab them with our stakes. My head pounds from my spent charms. I don't know how many more vampires are coming, but their number seems infinite. Sweat tracks down my back, and over my forehead and temples. I'm breathing hard. Boone fights off to the side, as vampires approach him one after another, their movements quick.

I risk a glance behind me and I'm dismayed to see more figures approaching through the darkness.

"They're trying to surround us," I gasp.

Carson turns his head, sees the newcomers from the corner of his eye. "There's too many of them."

"I know." We're going to have to retreat, although I

don't see any way out of this tunnel, not with the vampires approaching from all sides.

This ain't exactly how I expected to fall into a grave, but I suppose, given my occupation, it ain't much of a surprise.

The tunnel's filled with the sick crunch of bones and the eerie green light of our charms. My pistol's empty and there's no way to take a break from the onslaught of vampires to reload it. One of Boone's opponents shrieks as Boone embeds a stake in its heart. The vampire closest to me lunges, its fists curled into talons and a cruel smile on its face. I widen my stance and get ready to fight it with a grimace of my own.

Boone slays two vampires on his way over to us. "We'll work together," he says. "Three of us, our backs together."

Fighting a horde of bloodthirsty vampires, with another vampire at my back? A week ago—hell, a day ago—the idea would've sounded preposterous. But right now, there's nothing I'd like better.

A vampire jumps at me and I puncture its chest cavity with my stake.

"Let's do it," I say, immediately putting my back to Boone and Carson so the three of us form a tight triangle. Even as I do so, the horde is surrounding us.

Either they wear us down and we make a mistake and die, or we prevail.

My muscles want to seize up, tired from the exertion of fighting so many without a reprieve. Just how many were accumulated into this nest? They formed an army.

If we can't kill them, they'll surely overtake Penance, and it won't even be hard for them.

My arms move automatically, and I try not to think of how tired they're becoming. My head pounds, like my brain's too big for my skull. Fear and rage fuel me in equal measures. A vampire approaches, and I'm almost too slow to track it. A long scratch appears on my arm. I question how it got there. The vampire. It was faster than I could even see. It does it again, on my left arm, then reaches for the stake I hold in my left hand.

I let it have that stake but at the same time jab upward with the stake in my right hand. My forearm stings and throbs with pain, but I send the stake home into the vampire's heart.

It falls to the ground, legs askew, against the pile of other bodies I've fought off.

No more vampires approach. I peer into the darkness. Have we finally exhausted their army? I know I'm exhausted. My arms feel limp. It's all I can do to hold the last stake in my hand. I turn to see how Boone and Carson are faring.

Boone and the last vampire are facing off. Of course it comes down to this—John Marlowe, the vampire with the high forehead and pointed beard.

Carson pivots to help, so I look farther into the shadows of the mine. A strange shape looms in the darkness and I start toward it slowly, caution in every footstep.

The mine doesn't tunnel through like I'd thought it would—it collapsed at some point and is completely blocked. It's a relief—there won't be an unending horde of bloodsuckers advancing out of the darkness. The ones we fought—and there were many—were all there is.

But the shape against the side of the tunnel wall still puzzles me. Maybe my sight charm was cracked in the skirmish, I'm not sure.

I step closer, then gasp when I realize what I'm looking at. Three people are manacled to the wall, arms out at their sides, heads hanging forward.

Moving to the closest one, a young man, I press my hand against the fresh wounds in his neck. Still warm. The man looks at me, eyes wide. "Run," he gasps.

"It's safe now," I say, turning to see Boone thrust his stake into the heart of the last vampire. John Marlowe is deader than dead. Relief washes through me. "We're safe."

The man follows my gaze and sags in relief. Blood drips from one of his hands, sticky and dark, probably from him trying to protect himself.

"Those other two," I say, pointing to the folks next to him, "do you know if they're still alive?"

"I think they are," he says.

His manacles aren't locked, merely latched in a way that he wouldn't be able to unfasten them on his own. I free each of his wrists and he falls forward to his knees.

"Thank you," he says over and over again. "Thank you, thank you."

Feeling uncomfortable with the effusive gratitude, and wanting nothing more than to lie down and let my charm-created headache pass, I move over to the next captive, a red-haired woman. From the color of her dress and the fabric we found when we found the brothers, I assume she's Mrs. Browning's daughter, whose name escapes me. She moans faintly as I unfasten her mana-cles, and Carson rushes over to catch her when she falls forward. He sets her gently on the ground next to the first man.

I free the third person, another young man who has the same red hair as the young woman, and Carson catches him as he did the woman.

Boone's cutting off the heads of the fallen vampires while I try to wake the unconscious woman and man.

"What are their names?" I ask the first man.

He shakes his head. "They never said."

I shake the woman's shoulder. Her eyes briefly open before rolling closed again. Savage bite marks cover her neck. If she survives this, she'll have scars forever, scars much worse than the one on my neck from where Pa bit me.

"Hey," I say. "Hey, wake up."

Carson's trying to wake the unconscious man, who has similar wounds on his neck. "It's no use," he finally says. "He's not waking up, not anytime soon. We'll have to carry these two out of here."

Three of them, three of us, and three horses. Not ideal, but we'll make it work.

Boone's made quick work of the vampire heads. He strides over, wiping his knife on his pants. His hands are covered in blood, and a quickly healing gash crosses his neck to his collarbone, dipping below a tear in his shirt.

I don't care about the blood. I don't care about the barely-restrained fury still shining in his eyes.

I don't care that he's a vampire.

Reaching forward, I open my arms and pull him toward me.

He stumbles at first, surprised probably, but then his arms come around my back and he holds me tightly.

"I'm sorry," I whisper.

"I know," he says. "It's all right, Gracie."

It's the first time he's called me by my first name. I don't know what it means. Friendship? I don't feel I deserve such an overture, but I will surely grab it with both hands and hang on for dear life.

Someone coughs gently, and I look down to see the first man I freed from the wall. He says, "Apologies, but I'm hoping we can leave here soon?"

"Of course," I say, reluctantly letting go of Boone. There's more to say to him, more I want to hear, too. I'm not sure exactly what, yet, but it's there between us, waiting.

TWENTY-FIVE

HEAD POUNDING, I go out to Kitty and find some burlap sacks in one of the saddlebags, as well as some mending stones. They aren't as powerful as the healing charm around my wrist, but the three survivors won't need anything much stronger—if they'll even accept these. Bringing the bags back into the mine, I begin gathering heads. It's too dark to make out features of the individual vampires, and I no longer know who's on that wanted poster and who ain't. I gather a few of the heads and leave the rest.

The body of the newest vampire, Beatrice, is the last one I come to. Setting down my sack, I go back to Kitty and retrieve my short spade. The grave I dig is too shallow to really be called a grave, but it's all I can manage. The sooner we get the living back to their town, the better off they'll be. Food, water, and healing charms or medicine is what they need.

Through the fog of my charm-induced headache, I invoke three mending stones. Two of them I slip them into the pockets of the two unconscious survivors. Carson and Boone help the unconscious folks onto Carson's and my horses. The wounds on their necks are pink and raw, but not outright bleeding. The third guy, who says his name is Nicholas, is the one with the newer wounds, but they look shallow and he ain't complaining, although he asks politely for a bandana. Carson hands him one, and he wraps it around his neck with a word of thanks. He also accepts my third mending stone with a nod of thanks.

We get on our horses. Kitty and I lead the way, with the unconscious man sitting in front of me. Boone rides on Pegasus, with Nicholas riding behind him. Carson has the unconscious woman in front of him on his saddle.

The horses make their steady way along the trail. The bags of heads clunk against Kitty's flank, so I adjust them a little so they won't stain her coat with blood.

Moonlight surrounds us, illuminating our path through the brush and the dry, gnarled trees. I take in a deep breath of the night air, feel my shoulders relax. I have new vampire scars on my neck to add to my old one. Maybe they won't be so bad, maybe they'll heal up cleaner. I doubt it, but I don't much care either way.

It finally sinks in that we did it. We killed the vampires. We have the heads, we'll get the bounty—enough gold to give me and Kitty a nice, long break somewhere quiet. I picture that little ranch I stopped at for a rest on my way to Penance. Someplace like that, with some pretty wildflowers. Maybe a stream nearby. And I'll have plenty of fresh bread to throw into it, instead of hardtack.

My head might feel like horses have stomped it well and good, after all those charms I slung around in that mine, but we did it. Our job is done.

The man in front of me stirs.

"Hey," I say. "What's your name?"

"Jacob." His voice is so faint, I can barely hear him. He turns in the seat to look behind us, nearly loses his balance. "Where's Ellamae?"

"Just behind me," I say. "She's with Carson, and Nicholas is with Boone."

He goes stiff in front of me, and I flick a glance to his eyes, which are hard as he looks past Carson and Ellamae to Boone and Nicholas. "He's a...he's a vampire."

"He is," I say, understanding the impulse to judge him a monster—I did for a spell, too. "But he's not like the rest. Boone's...different."

"Not Boone," Jacob gasps. "Nicholas. He's the leader. He fed on Ellamae, knocked her out. Did the same to me just after he clawed at his own neck."

My whole body goes cold. I turn in my saddle.

Nicholas has his arm around Boone's neck. A stake is in his other hand and he presses it into Boone's chest.

Nicholas was the faceless, nameless leader of the nest.

I reach for my pistol, but it's out of charms. The only thing I have is my last stake. It's been spelled for accuracy, but Boone's in front of Nicholas. I don't have a good opening for staking Nicholas; what would likely happen is I stake Boone. And I can't do that. I won't.

Nicholas smiles, revealing the fangs I didn't see when we were in the mine. That face of his can look like anything, it's so bland. It ain't round nor square nor long. It ain't dark nor light. No wonder the artist for the wanted poster couldn't draw it; there ain't nothing distinctive about it.

Nicholas says, "You can't win, little charmslinger. I'm going to kill your pet vampire."

"Let him go," I say.

"Drop the pistol and the stake," Nicholas says, his voice a hiss.

I let go of the stake and it lands on the saddle between Jacob and me. My mind's going fast, thoughts muddling together, tripping over each other. I get dozens of ideas and discard each of them just as quickly as they come.

Then I drop the pistol. It falls to the dirt at Kitty's hooves. Pointing to my pistol on the ground, I say, "Look, I did what you wanted. See?"

The vampire flicks its gaze to the ground, and I use its distraction and whisper to Jacob, "Stake's right behind you. Can you throw?"

The words are so quiet, just a breath against his ear. He nods.

"What do you want?" I ask Nicholas.

"I *wanted* a town. But I'll settle with a snack and an escape, for now," he says.

He wants to get away so he can rebuild his army. In a year, or five, or ten, or twenty, he'll be back at Penance or another Rift town, ready to take it over and fulfill his goal of a vampire town.

"Give me the girl and a horse, and I'll let your precious vampire pet go," he says.

"Don't do it," Boone says. "I'm not worth that. Let him kill me, then you kill him."

Carson, who's been frozen up until now with his hand on his holster, says, "Don't be ridiculous, Boone."

Boone shakes his head slightly. "I mean it. I'm already dead, Gracie."

"He's got a point," Carson says.

"Close your mouth, Carson," I say.

He snaps it shut, but I can see his hand hovering over that pistol of his. Carson's thinking about killing them both, and the thought sends a flare of anger through me.

"Come now, Gracie." Nicholas's voice is conciliatory, his smile full of empty promises. "Nobody has to die. The girl comes with me. You keep your vampire pet. I live to continue my miserable existence with only the girl for company."

I wish the sun would rise, burn this vampire out of our midst. But it's hours until dawn.

"You can't have the girl," I say.

Nicholas's stake digs harder into Boone's chest. It's hard to get a clear visual from here, but I can see Boone's face tighten in pain.

"I can't have the girl," Nicholas says slowly.

"No, you can't." Hands up, I slide from Kitty's saddle. "But you can have me."

Boone and Carson immediately begin to argue, but I shake my head.

"I'm coming," I say. "I left the stake there, see?"

Nicholas's focus moves to where I point, the saddle where I'd been sitting, the stake behind Jacob. And Jacob, for his part, is slumped forward, head turned slightly to see what's happening, but for all appearances too weak to hold himself up. I'm counting on the hope that he ain't too weak to throw that stake.

Boone shakes his head. "Don't do this, Gracie."

"No other option," I say.

"Stand there," Nicholas says, pointing to a spot next to Pegasus.

I stop where he told me and look up with expectation. "Now what?"

I can see his mind working, as he tries to figure out the best way to let Boone go and still reach me. I can see the moment he realizes that there's no graceful way to do this. I can see the moment he realizes there's no winning.

"Now, Jacob," I shout.

I grab Boone's leg and yank him from the saddle just as Jacob turns, grabs the stake, and flings it at Nicholas.

The stake, charmed for speed, force, and accuracy, *misses*. It hits Nicholas in the chest, but not the heart.

He bellows in rage.

Boone falls on top of me and we land in a heap in the dirt. Pegasus rears, dislodging Nicholas, who falls heavily to the ground a few feet away.

I crawl out from under Boone and over to Nicholas's side. Nicholas reaches for me.

The stream is no more than a yard away.

Neither Carson nor I made an offering on our way up this hill.

I bet Nicholas didn't make any offerings, either.

On all fours, I place myself between the vampire and the stream. From the corner of my eye I see something—a big arm, the hand looking like it's been dipped in red, looking like it's way too big to be submerged in such a trickle of water.

Nicholas yanks the stake from his chest, and those cruel eyes glitter. Nicholas crawls toward me.

Boone and Carson are shouting, Boone's struggling to reach for his pistol and I imagine Carson is getting ready to shoot, too. But there's no time.

Nicholas leaps forward and I jerk myself sideways, out of the vampire's reach at the same time that red-tipped hand extends fully out of the water and grabs the first fleshy being within reach—Nicholas.

The vampire screams and claws at the arm, but it's no match for the fae. I remember Sheriff and Carson telling us about their nightmares, the fae battling the vampires. Hardin wondering aloud who would win.

Turns out, the fae would win.

The first fae arm is joined by a coiling second, something with too many joints to be human, like an arm with several elbows. I don't know if the vampire's shrieking is angering the fae or what, but it uses that second arm to rip the vampire's head clean off its body.

Then it quickly drags both parts into the stream, where everything disappears.

Finally, Nicholas is deader than dead.

I round on Boone, who's beginning to sit up, and I shove him back down. As he blinks up at me from his spot in the dirt, I shout, "What in the hell were you thinking? You're *not worth it*? You're *already dead*?"

"I *am* a vampire," he says with a shrug.

"And a fool one at that," I say, "if you can't tell you're also my friend."

I stand up, then extend a hand toward him. He clasps it and I pull him up, not that he really needs my help.

Once he's up, I dash the tears from my cheeks with the back of my hand and pull him into a hug.

And I don't think to myself that I'm hugging a vampire. I think, *I'm hugging a friend.*

TWENTY-SIX

AS WE RIDE TOWARD PENANCE, I have all manner of questions for Levi Boone rattling around in my brainpan. That his lightbending charm and whatever glamour he's using got past my own sight charm is easy enough to figure—the magic he's using must be powerful strong. With the bounty from this hunt, I'll invest in an even stronger sight charm so this kind of thing can't slip past me in the future.

What I really want to know is, how come he ain't a monster.

Jacob's asleep again, even as we ride. He lists one way, then the other, and I hold him in place much as I can. Carson's doing the same with Ellamae. Boone's at my side, and his lips quirk up ever so slightly in a smile when I give a grunt of effort to keep Jacob from falling off the saddle.

"I reckon you have questions for me," Boone says in a soft voice.

"Just one," I say.

"Is it the fangs?" he asks.

"No, a strong glamour'll hide those easy enough."

He nods. "Is it the diet, then?"

"No," I say in surprise. I hadn't gotten that far in my wonderings.

"Really. Huh," he says. "I thought it would've been your first question after the fangs."

"I reckon you eat or drink whatever you need and you get by somehow," I say, figuring out the solution as I say the words. "It ain't important to me so long as you ain't killing innocents."

He shakes his head and his brown eyes are serious. "I ain't killing innocents."

I do wonder, now, whether he drinks blood, and if so, where he gets it from. Especially as we just spent several days together and I didn't see him take a sip of it at any time. But that ain't the question plaguing me.

"So what is it you want to know?" he asks.

I hesitate, using the need for adjusting Jacob's posture as an excuse not to speak right away. I'm not sure how to properly word my thoughts. Boone's patient while he waits, his face easy and relaxed as the horses' movements.

Eventually, I say, "You're an outlaw, but not."

"Here I thought you'd have practical questions, and you've gone all philosophical on me," he says.

"Nothing philosophical about this," I say. "My pa, the sweetest man who ever lived, turned into a vampire. I had to stake my own pa. How come he didn't turn out like you?"

"I'm sorry, Gracie," he says. "I don't rightly know."

He rides on ahead, and the puzzled expression I

caught on his face matches my own thoughts.

It's midday by the time we reach Penance. The City of Silver is subdued, no doubt in part from seeing Hardin's and Sheriff's empty mounts coming in before us.

Wesley's waiting by the church, sitting on top of a large rock in the shade of a giant mesquite. He looks up when we approach, scans our faces. My heart squeezes in my chest, sadness making it tight.

"How'd she go?" he asks.

"She went as a hero," I say shortly.

"I want the details. I want to know everything."

"I'll tell you everything you want to know," I say. "Boone, Carson, will you take care of the heads, and the Brownings, and the horses?"

"Got it," Carson says, while Boone nods.

I climb down from Kitty and stand next to Wesley's rock. Wesley and I watch the others go, the sun bright on their hats and shoulders. Ellamae's arms are sunburned, but not too bad. Mostly, she and Jacob need water, food, and the love of their grieving mother. I hope they're able to get well, and revive their brother Bill.

Jacob, for his part, has agreed to keep Boone's preternatural status a secret. "He ain't harming people, then I don't consider him an outlaw," Jacob said, in a brilliant, nonjudgmental way that made me feel ashamed of myself for doubting Boone all over again.

I scramble up onto the boulder with Wesley. Sitting there in the shade, I answer all of his questions, taking him through his ma's death, explaining how I tried to save her.

He looks pointedly at my wrist, at the third strand of beads there.

"My friends wouldn't let me use it," I say. "She was already gone. I tried to, but they stopped me."

He's quiet. Wipes his face with his palm, scratches that baby of a mustache gracing his upper lip. "I reckon you did more than anyone else could've expected, with those other two charms."

"I can't tell you how much I wish they'd worked," I say. "But healing charms don't work when a soul's already left the body."

"And what'd you do with her body?"

"Buried her. It's not a beautiful grave, but we rolled a big rock over it, to keep the critters from disturbing her rest."

He nods. "Tell me about Hardin. He's dead, too?"

I hesitate. I don't know how much to reveal.

Wesley nods, as if my silence confirms something for him. "We already found he'd been taking payments from the outlaws. His wife found a letter and gold. She didn't understand it, brought it to me. I'm not sure I understand it, to be honest."

"I'm sorry," I say, and explain Hardin's side of the tale.

"He's responsible for my ma's death," Wesley says. "I only wish I could kill him."

I nod. "Boone had that honor, though. I'd kill him a second time if I could."

"I'm thinking, maybe his widow don't need to know about his part in the tale." Wesley's looking at me with a clear expression of hope and empathy in his face.

"I'm thinking I agree with you on that," I say, calling to mind Mrs. Hardin's cheery demeanor and friendly chatting while she served coffee and breakfast. That morning seems about a century ago.

"Do you think Boone and Carson would be likeminded?"

Nodding, I say, "I suspect so." Then I add, "Hardin doesn't deserve that kindness."

"No, he doesn't," Wesley agrees. "But his widow and his little boy don't deserve whatever scorn this Rift town would heap on 'em. They'd be considered guilty just for being relations of the two-faced traitor. And it's hard enough saying goodbye to someone you love. At least I have the comfort of knowing my ma was a hero."

I don't think of myself as very physical, but I reach out and take his hand and give it a gentle squeeze. Because that's what his ma would want. "She was a hero. I admired her greatly, and still do."

Scrubbing a hand over his eyes, Wesley says, "Well. Well."

I give him a moment to collect himself, send my gaze down the long street going through the center of Penance. Silver glints from accents on the false storefronts, dust kicks up behind a man driving a wagon. It ain't a bad place, other than its proximity to the Rift.

"Well." Wesley clears his throat. "I suppose a celebration of some kind is in order. It would be my ma organizing it, as the sheriff, but as we don't have a sheriff right now, I'd like to take on that responsibility."

I'd thought he was just a young upstart when I first met him. But Wesley's got some deeper layers to him.

"A celebration don't feel right," I say. "Not with your ma dying. We'll accept some food, maybe, and get along on our way."

He shakes his head. "We can honor my mom...and Hardin, I s'pose, while celebrating that the nest is gone. There'll be a town feast tonight, Miss Boswell, and I truly hope you and your posse will join us."

I've never agreed to come to a town feast, not once in my nine years hunting bounties. But Wesley's so genuine, and I find I wouldn't be averse to drinking a toast to his ma's life, and celebrating a job well done.

"Thank you," I say. "I'll be there."

"Good. Now let's go to the bank and retrieve your bounty."

———

IT'S a bright afternoon when the large tables come out to the street. Penance residents arrange them in the shade and begin carrying dishes and platters of food out. I help whenever I can. Boone hurries after Mrs. Hardin out of the saloon, each of them balancing trays laden with drink.

I met with Boone and Carson briefly, after going to the bank with Wesley, and divided up the bounty between us. It's the biggest take I've ever gotten from a hunt, even after the split. It'll replace my healing charms, purchase a new bridle for Kitty, and maybe I'll even have some left over to save. I still haven't forgotten my vision of a little farmhouse in the valley.

Finally, the meal is ready. I find myself seated between Wesley and Carson. On Carson's other side is his pa, a man with a twinkle in his blue eyes almost as handsome as his son's. Across from us sit Boone, Mrs. Hardin, and her son. Both Mrs. Hardin and the boy have red-rimmed eyes. Boone talks quietly with them, and even coaxes a smile out of the boy.

None of the townspeople seem to know that Boone's a vampire—Jacob Browning really is keeping the secret. Boone's accepted here. The thought of it makes my heart warm.

Mrs. Browning sits a few seats down with Jacob, Ella-mae, and Bill close to her. Bill doesn't talk, but he eats. It looks like he'll eventually get better, and I'm grateful. No soul should have to live in that kind of waking nightmare that kept him still and quiet.

The meal is good, which I register on a logical, factual level. My enjoyment is tempered by my wish that Sheriff were here, and I reckon a lot of the folk gathered around the table feel the same. I take a large swig of the liquid in the mug in front of me. I'm not sure what it is, but it surely ain't water. Sweet, alcoholic, and body-warming.

It gives me the courage I need. This is the last time I'll see all of these people, anyhow. Standing, I say, "I ain't one for speeches. But I want to say that I usually work alone. This particular hunt was complicated and danger-ous. We lost good people—great people. I couldn't have done it without a single one of them. Thank you for the feast."

Several of the townspeople clap, including my posse. There's probably more I should say, like talking about Boone's honor, Carson's growing bravery, Sheriff's hero-ism, and to whatever extent I feel like lying, Hardin's assistance in the venture. But my face is burning from the booze and the attention, so I sit my ass down and finish my meal, not looking up.

There ain't much left on my plate, and I push it around as I think about where I'll go next.

Once every bit of food and drink on the tables has been consumed, the music starts, piano notes streaming from the nearby saloon along with an accompanying fiddle. A young woman tugs Carson off the bench so he can dance, and Boone's deep in conversation with Hardin's boy sitting next to him.

I turn to Wesley and shake his hand. "I think that means it's about time for me to head out. Thank you kindly for the feast and the company."

My body's eager to move, to get out again. I'll visit Kitty, make sure she's rested enough for a journey, and then find the nearest witch.

It's back to my old patterns. The disruption of the feast has been enough excitement for a lifetime. Glancing one last time at Boone and Carson, I realize they have their own lives, just as I have mine. Nobody promised more, and I pushed them away at every turn. They couldn't possibly want to continue on as we were.

This feast was just as much a way of saying goodbye to the townspeople as it was a way of saying goodbye to them.

There's a pang, a sorrowful grip on my heart, but I breathe through it and make my way down the dusty street as twilight falls.

Farewells are a part of life. If they didn't make me sad, I'd be a true outlaw.

TWENTY-SEVEN

THE WITCH'S charm shop smells like every other witch's charm shop—chalk, scented oils, and a nostril-assaulting mix of herbs. The witch behind the counter eyes me coolly over a teacup as she takes a sip. Her dark eyebrows don't move, giving me no hint as to her true feelings. She could just as easily be excited about having a customer as disgusted by humans who sling charms.

I remove my hat and make my way toward her.

"What can I do for you?" she asks in an even voice.

"Looking to replenish some charms," I say. The gold Wesley gave me is in my coat, weighing down the pocket.

The witch sets down her cup and turns to the shelves behind the counter. "You a bounty hunter?" she asks over her shoulder.

"I am."

"You'll want healing charms, some general accuracy and strength charms, and some charmed stakes as well, if I am not mistaken?"

"That's correct, ma'am."

She bustles around behind the counter, opening drawers, slamming them shut. She lifts a giant tray and brings it over to the counter so I can peruse the offerings she thinks I'd be most interested in.

The door opens behind me, and I turn.

Boone and Carson walk in, deep in conversation. My heart jumps into my throat. I'm not sure what they're doing in here. Casual browsing, this late in the afternoon?

They haven't seen me. Heads bent toward each other as they speak in low voices, they make their way over to the wall of wanted posters.

I turn back to the witch. She wrinkles her nose at their rudeness for walking in without so much as a tip of the hat or a muttered *good evening*. Me, I'm grateful they haven't spied me. With any luck, I'll gather my charms, pay the witch, and skedaddle out of here before I have to speak to them.

While I run my fingers over some of the stakes piled in the far slot of the witch's tray, I pick up some of what Boone and Carson are saying.

"This hunt looks like at least a two-person job," Carson says.

"Three would be better." Boone's voice is still low, but it carries over to me, like I'm extra attuned to his register.

"Well, we don't have three." Carson's boot hits the floor to punctuate that statement. I can imagine him frowning as he squints at the different posters. "Maybe we should do it anyway."

"I reckon we could try," Boone says. "Take down the poster, Carson. Two people it is. Against a nest of...wow, that's a big number."

"Aw, seven vampires shouldn't be so hard, not after what we just did."

Seven vampires? Have they lost their minds?

"I reckon you're right," Boone agrees. "Should take us a day to find 'em and take 'em out."

"That's it." I spin around on my boot heels and face them. "You're going to get yourselves killed is what you're going to do."

Instead of frowning at me, or looking surprised at my outburst, they're both smirking, and they exchange a knowing look.

"What are you smiling about?" I demand.

"That was some expert manipulation right there," the witch says behind me, and then she laughs.

I shoot her a glance before turning back to the men. "You knew I was in here?"

"Followed you here," Carson says proudly. "You didn't even notice."

No, I didn't notice. I was feeling too sorry for myself.

Boone strides over, a wanted poster in his hand. He spreads it out over an open space on the worn wooden counter. From the paper, three vampires stare sullenly up at us. The job's in Halo, which is a lot farther south, a four- or five-day ride.

"I thought you said seven vampires," I say.

Boone just chuckles, and the corners of his caramel eyes crinkle. "What do you say, Boswell? Will you hunt another bounty with us?"

I open my mouth, close it. They want me to join them? My throat feels too full to talk, so I just nod. After a moment, I force out the words, "We split the bounty even between the three of us, just like this time."

Carson nods and Boone says, "Of course. Wouldn't have it any other way. We're partners."

Partners.

Carson sticks out a hand. I eye it for a minute, like it might bite me, but I know Carson. I've seen his honesty and bravery. He stuck by me when even *I* didn't want to stick by me. So I shake his hand.

Boone holds out his hand next. A vampire—for a partner. I never would've thought. Yet he is truer and better than some humans I can think of. He doesn't have to prove himself to me ever again. I know who he is, inside. I shake his hand, too.

"Partners," I say.

The witch clears her throat. "So are you all just standing around gabbing, or are you going to buy some magic?"

———

LESS THAN AN HOUR LATER, Boone, Carson, and I are on our horses, heading south, the open desert prairie lit by moonlight.

———

THE SECOND BOOK IN THE CHARMSLINGER

SERIES, *BLOOD BEAST*, WILL BE RELEASED IN FEBRUARY 2021!

She pushes me down and I fly backward, arms scrambling for leverage or support. Nothin'. I fall onto my ass and she's on top of me, faster'n I would've thought possible, her steely fingers hooked on my elbows while her wiry body settles on my stomach.

"I've got you now, charmslinger. You stay away from Carson."

"He's a little young for you, don't you think?"

Ire flashes in her eyes and she spits as she says, "You know nothin'. That's why I'm on top."

I nod, which is a mite awkward as I'm flat on my back. "You're right about one thing, wrong about the other."

Her anger don't diminish, merely transforms to a sneering scowl as she tries to work out the puzzle. Giving up, she snarls, "How d'you figure?"

"I know nothing, you're right about that," I say before lifting my legs and bucking her over my head.

She crashes into the wall, limbs askew. She curses as she pushes herself up to sitting.

I continue, "But you're wrong about bein' on top."

Unholstering my pistol, I train it on her while I find my hat from where she knocked it to the floor.

A spot of blood wells where her lip got cut in the fall. I imagine I look a touch worse—my left eye is already starting to swell. No problem, I aim with my right.

Carson told me she would help. Looks like he don't know shapeshifters any better'n I do.

———

VISIT   HTTPS://LIZASTREETAUTHOR.COM/
BLOOD-BEAST for details on how to get your copy of
Blood Beast.

ALSO BY LIZA STREET

Spellbound Shifters: Dragons Entwined

(with Keira Blackwood)

Dragon Forgotten (a FREE prequel)

Dragon Shattered

Dragon Unbroken

Dragon Reborn

Dragon Ever After

———

Spellbound Shifters: Fates and Visions

(with Keira Blackwood)

Oracle Defiant

Oracle Adored

Spellcaster Hidden

———

Spellbound Shifters Standalones

(with Keira Blackwood)

Hope Reclaimed

Orphan Entangled

———

Alphas & Alchemy: Fierce Mates

(with Keira Blackwood)

Claimed in Forbidden

Fated in Forbidden

Bound to Forbidden

Caught in Forbidden

Mated in Forbidden

Forever in Forbidden

.

ABOUT LIZA

Liza likes her heroes packing muscles and her heroines packing agency. She got her start in romance by sneak-reading her grandma's paperbacks. Now she's a *USA Today* bestselling author and she spends her time writing about hot shifters with fierce and savage hearts.

Join Liza's mailing list to get all the good news when it happens! Visit https://lizastreetauthor.com/free-book/